THE SAGA of

ARGO

THE SAGA of GRITTEL SUNDOTHA

GRITTEL SUNDOTHA

by **Ardath Mayhar**

ATHENEUM   *1985*   New York

Chapter III, *Gritellia, Sorceress,* appeared
in *Dragonfields* #4, Winter 1983 issue,
copyright © 1983 by Ardath Mayhar.

Chapter II, *Who Courts a Reluctant Maiden,* appeared
in slightly different form in AMAZONS II, anthology
published by DAW Books, copyright © 1982
by Ardath Mayhar.

Library of Congress Cataloging in Publication Data

Mayhar, Ardath.
    The saga of Grittel Sundotha.

    "An Argo book."
    Summary: After rejecting her only likely proposal of
marriage, seven-foot Grittel wanders the kingdom using
her strength and skill to right wrongs until she goes on
a quest and finds her true destiny.
    [1. Fantasy. 2. Size—Fiction] I. Title.
PZ7.M468Sag 1985   [Fic]   84-21523
ISBN 0-689-31097-8

Published simultaneously in Canada by
McClelland & Stewart, Ltd.
Composition by Maryland Linotype, Baltimore, Maryland
Printed and bound by Fairfield Graphics, Fairfield, Pennsylvania
Designed by Signature Graphics
First Edition

To

ANDRE NORTON,
*who has spurred my imagination
to greater heights.*

CONTENTS

THE SAGA of GRITTEL SUNDOTHA

тHE LAST
of sundoth

I should have known something was afoot when my father called me from the fields early. I had been supervising the removal of stubble and sprouts from last year's crops and planning, as I went along, the placements of the new year's plantings. Not unimportant work, as he well knew. He had not interrupted me in the fields since I was fourteen and took on the oversight of his farming.

The bailiff came after me. His manner was that mixture of feigned humility and secret contempt that I particularly disliked in him. He could not swallow the fact that I, a woman, understood the working of the farm better than he. And, far worse, that I also overtopped his considerable height by more than a foot. The combination set his teeth on edge, a matter that I would have done all I could to ease, if he had done the same. Unfortunately, he did not. I took wicked delight in making his lot harder.

Still, though I managed to tease him a bit on our way across the fields toward Sundoth Keep, my mind was not entirely occupied with that. I had noted, all winter, covert glances from my mother toward my father, then toward me. I knew her well. Enough to understand that she had something in her mind that she was set upon. And I also recognized plainly the fact that she regarded my existence as an obstacle in the way of favorable marriages for my four sisters, all of whom are of normal size and quite pretty, as I am most certainly not. So I had some reason for my unease, which grew greater as we came near the walls of Sundoth.

"You may go about your duties now, Arek," I told the bailiff. We had reached the portal leading into the walled back garden. "I am not so frail that I need your guardianship to the very door." I grinned at him. He flushed to the roots of his sand-colored hair. I could feel waves of hatred coming from him.

Once inside the garden I forgot him, however. A large coach had been pulled up into the stable yard. Several horses could be heard stamping about beyond the wall that enclosed the horse-close. I had not known that visitors were expected. It was rare indeed for any to arrive unannounced, for roads had become rough, in these late years, and highwaymen and other unsavory characters abounded. Curiosity sent me hurrying to my room to wash and change to a gown from my rough farm-wear. My mother would have spit prickles if I had appeared in company dressed in man's garb.

I owned one decent gown. Though my sisters teased constantly for materials in order to make fanciful whimsies to cover their nakedness, I had neither the need nor the desire for such things. My mother had forced this gown upon me, and I hated it with pent-up passion. It was yellow, which turned my tanned complexion to mud, and it fitted me closely, which was worse.

Not that there is anything wrong with my shape. There's the rub. My face and my height call for the build of a stable-hand. Unfortunately, I am finely proportioned, for all my seven-foot frame, and unmistakably female. If there is anything that I abhor, it is having all the men of my acquaintance, including my grandsir's peers, look no higher than my collar-bone when they talk with me. Even if I am sitting down.

I donned the hated garment with distaste, brushed my hair, and pinned it up again into severe braids. I knew that Mother would go tight-lipped at that, but I refused to puff and curl it. Then I stood to look into the tall mirror that faced one wall of my room.

Agh! I preferred my guise as a farmhand.

Nevertheless, I knew that I must not take too long in coming down. Mother would send someone after me soon. I pulled on slippers, scowled at my reflection, and went downstairs.

It was worse than anything I could have anticipated. The hall was filled with chattering, screaming, fighting brats. This was particularly distressing since my folk, like most, had brought their children up to a pattern of strict decorum, in company or out. These hellions, both male and female, seemed bent upon bringing down the roof about our ears.

I looked across the teeming floor toward the great chairs beside the hearth, where the parents of these untaught offspring must be sitting, in company with my own. A man sat in the guest-chair nearest the fire. No woman except for my mother was there. Something like an alarm-bell rang sharply in my brain.

I managed to make my way to my own chair without being tripped or deafened by any of the young ones . . . only to find that not one of my sisters was in attendance. The tall backs of the chairs, as I passed, revealed empty seats. Another bell sounded.

The man was old. Of course, I was very young. Anyone above the age of thirty seemed ancient to me then, but this man was gray of hair and wrinkled of brow. Ill-tempered gray eyes peered out between thickets of horn-like eyebrows. And he looked once at my face, grimaced slightly, and turned his gaze downward. My temper began to simmer.

Mother rose to take my hand. She turned us toward the man. "Dom Lekker, this is our daughter, Grittellia Floresca, eldest child of Sundoth. Grittel, this gentleman is the holder of Garnim Keep, four days' journey to the east. He has done us the immense honor of coming here in order to offer for your hand. I trust that you will behave with proper decorum."

There was a strong warning in her words.

I caught my father's eye as I went forward to curtsy.

He blushed and looked down. I felt for him. He had been maneuvered, I knew immediately, into something that suited him very ill, indeed. Before I had grown to an age to manage the farms, he had done very badly at it. He would miss more than my company, if I left the hold.

Dom Lekker did not have the courtesy to rise. I began to see just where his children got their lack of manners. He took my hand in a damp grip, pulled me forward in order that he might touch it to his lips, then dropped it hastily.

"Your father tells me that you are an excellent manager of his agriculture. That is a valuable skill, but are you also skilled in household matters?"

I looked him in the eye. "Having sisters who are unfit for field work, I have left such matters to them," I said firmly. "Sewing, cookery, and management of house servants are not attributes for which I have any need. Nor the rearing of children." I glanced aside at one young scamp who had taken a decorative blade from the wall and was laying about him. I hoped he would behead at least one of his siblings before it was taken away.

The Dom frowned. He looked at me again (from the neck downward, of course). He nodded toward my father. "She is bright and can learn what is needful. And she is large enough to knock some manners into the cubs. I'll take her, Sundoth."

My blood came to a boil. "You will take me? Indeed! But will I take you? Your manners are woefully in need of knocking about themselves. No wonder your children are such atrocities! I am no compliant chattel, sirrah. I am a competent woman, strong and self-willed enough to make my own way without the aid of any such graybeard as you. Even should I be fool enough to accept your offer, you would find that you had acquired much more than you bargained for. I would reorder much more about your household than your offspring. But I am not such a fool. I refuse your offer. Good day!" I turned upon my heel in one of the few graceful motions I have ever made and swept from the room, pushing before me a bow wave of brats. There were nine of them. I counted as I went.

I knew, of course, that I had altered, permanently and without hope of remedy, my relationship with my mother. She had lived for the day when she might remove my unbecoming presence from her household. There would be no more offers, I knew quite well. And, though my father must regret losing my skills and labors, he must live with Mother. That life would be total grief until my fate was settled, I knew.

Reaching my room, I removed the hated dress and stuffed it into the fire. In some way it symbolized the years of my childhood of obedience to my mother. The fields had been my refuge from her, always, and I returned there at once. Come what might, the plantings must be laid out, the field-folk instructed, and the bailiff prepared to take over upon my leaving. I would not leave my father, my sisters, or even my mother, whom I hated and loved, to suffer for want of what I could provide.

As I trudged back to my work I thought of the world outside the hold and its lands. It was not a comforting thought. Garetha's king, far away in his city on the seacoast, looked toward adventurings across the seas, leaving his country to become a shambles and losing the good order that his ancestors had imposed here. Now banditry and vicious witcheries played about the edges of the well-managed holds. The Visionaries were ignored, to a great extent, though their intuitions were valuable to those with the wit to pay heed to them.

Few travelers had come our way who had crossed to the other continents, that to the south and the other far to the east. But our tutor had been a man of great learning, and he had given us a good understanding of their conditions, as well as those of Garetha. More than one king went venturing there, and war rolled across those distant lands. It was not a world to beckon even a young man to adventuring.

The afternoon wore away slowly, but I threw my attention into my work and managed to lose the foreboding that stalked at my heels. Yet nightfall came, inexorably, and I turned, at last, back toward Sundoth. I knew what would await me there. I was not wrong.

My sister Betta, the only one with whom I had anything at all in common, was waiting for me outside the rear garden wall. Her gray cloak was nearly invisible against the stone, and I was startled when she reached forward and touched my shoulder.

"Oh, Grittel! What have you done? Mama is in a rage. Father looks as if someone has died. Our guests didn't even stay the night, and that is a shameful thing. And our sisters and the servants are buzzing with impossible tales. What has happened?"

I told her, as we crept in and up the stair to my room

without being detected. She was, as I had known she would be, horrified that anyone would or could defy her parents. "You would be cared for!" she cried. "There would be food and shelter and a place in your old age. You must think of such things, Grittel. How can you possibly survive, otherwise?"

"By my wits and my strong back," I said. I appreciated her concern, but she had no comprehension of what it means to be strong and large and independent. She never will, and I had no intention of upsetting the smooth course of her life with ambitions that she is not equipped to follow.

We went down together, which was brave of her. She understood quite well that Mother would find the opportunity to punish her for even that much indication of rebellion. The table was ablaze with lamps . . . burning the oil that my efforts had seen extracted from tala seeds. Around it sat five accusing faces.

There was nothing for it, now, but to carry on as if I had all the confidence in the world. I spoke to Father, to Mother, cast a general greeting toward my sisters, and slid into my place. The waiting soup had no flavor. I was not surprised. You might have sliced the tension in the air and served it as the main course.

It was Father's inflexible rule that nothing of import might be discussed before or during a meal. So it was that he asked me of the field-work, my sisters of their activities in the kitchen and sewing-room, my mother of her embroideries. The brief and absentminded replies he received did nothing to relieve the atmosphere of impending doom that lay upon the family. Even Mother seemed a bit subdued, and I felt sure that Father had explained to her how much of his present prosperity was attributable to my management of the farms. But I knew her too well to think that that might change her will. She brooked no questioning of her authority, even from Father.

Once the cloth was drawn, my sisters were sent, protesting, to their rooms. The three of us went into the hall and sat before the great fire, they on one side of the hearth, aligned against me. I took the bit in my teeth and spoke first.

"I know that you will be unwilling to harbor any who will not bow to your wills," I said, ostensibly to Father but actually to Mother. "I have taken that into account. I am quite willing to go away from Sundoth, taking only what is necessary for survival upon the road. I hope that you will not begrudge me that. If you are agreeable, I will stay to supervise the plantings. If not, I will instruct the bailiff. He is not entirely capable, but he can do it if he is properly guided. I would suggest replacing him, before another year, with old Hashom. He taught me most of what I know, and he should have been bailiff since Grandfather's death. I never understood why Arek was chosen."

Mother's eyes sparked, and I knew that he had been her choice. She seldom put any authority into the hands of the competent.

Before she could speak, I went on. "This is necessary, if you are not to lose the ground I have gained in the past five years. If you do not do that, there is actual want in your future. I cannot warn you strongly enough. If you want to make good matches for the girls, you must show a prosperous face to their suitors. Be warned on that point, if on no other." I could see the realization sink into my mother's mind. Her expression became thoughtful instead of hostile.

Father sighed heavily. "I would ask you to stay to see the spring work done, but that may not be." He glanced at Mother, and I knew precisely why it couldn't be. "We have looked into the accounts. We have considered the years of labor that you have done on behalf of the estate, and we have set aside a certain sum for you. It may seem over-generous" (Here he glared defiantly at Mother, who seemed slightly abashed) "but our well-being has rested upon your shoulders for years now. I can do no less. Your sisters will be well-portioned by your efforts. I will not have you less well provided for."

Mother blushed faintly.

"You . . . we have decided that, for the peace of mind of your sisters, it will be well if you go at once. After giving instructions for the plantings of course. I will leave you now to say goodbye to your mother." He didn't meet my eyes, though he kissed my cheek in an embarrassed manner. I thought I felt tears on his face.

Shocked to find that I now dared to put my true feelings into words, I turned to Mother. "You are a foolish woman. You value the trivial and hold worthless the valuable. You are so jealous of your authority that you make yourself ridiculous. Father would be a poor man, this moment, if I had not defied your wishes and taken the management of the farmsteads from his hands. He was glad to relinquish it, you may remember."

She looked up. Her face was red, this time with anger. "You see why I want you to go. Such sentiments are unbecoming a lady and a daughter. Your . . . attributes are not those I would have chosen. Your character is less than I tried to form. Your influence is well away from my daughters." She stood and set her hand into the cabinet of the tall desk beside her. "We have provided for you. There is enough silver in this bag to last for years, if you take care. What will become of you I do not know, and I find that I care very little."

"Whatever comes, it cannot but be a better fate than that of becoming wife to Lekker of Garnim and mother to his impossible children," I said. "Even you should have known that that was a bargain I would not keep."

She didn't comment upon that. "There is a pack made up for you. Clothing, equipment, food. I would prefer that you do not say goodbye to your sisters. It will upset them. I would like for you to be gone at first light. You rise early, so it will be no burden. By the time they come down, you must be gone from Sundoth."

"I pity them. They will live and die without knowing what it is to be a free being with mind and will of their own. You, of all women, should know the source of my self-will. Evidently, I got all that you had to pass on to your heirs, leaving them none. I prefer my fate to theirs." I stood and looked down at her from my great height.

"Goodbye, Mother. I will not say it again."

The next morning found me less confidently defiant. The dawn was chill, and frost rimed the stones of my father's wall as I opened a great panel and went out into the half-light. Behind me the sentinel whispered, "Good luck to ye, Grittellia Floresca." That was the only word I took with me from the house of my birth.

Yet there was one thing still to come. A final injury and insult, but one that gave some relief to my resentment and fury. Before I had gone a half-league, I heard a step behind me. There was no reason for any to travel so early, so I turned to look, and saw the familiar shape of Arek, together with two of his half-grown sons, striding after me.

"Do you bring a last word from my father?" I asked. Rather hopefully.

He laughed. "You are beyond your father's help, now. I have watched you for years, directing your betters, arrogant in your size. I have come to cut you down to the stature of any other woman. Grab her, my sons!"

I knew what he must mean. The fury that had boiled for a full night rose up in me, as the two young brutes set their hands upon me. I shook one off and kicked him senseless. Grasping the other behind the neck as if he were a puppy, I shook him briskly. His teeth literally rattled in his head. Then I dropped him and turned to Arek.

"I have wanted to thrash you since first I worked with you. I would not have been justified in doing that to my father's bailiff, so I abstained. Now look to yourself!" I cried.

He drew a long dagger from his belt and dropped into a fighting stance. I was surprised that he had even so much knowledge of the craft. But I had been taught more things than simple agriculture by Hashom. I struck out with my knobstick, and the blade went flying.

He backed a step, his eyes suddenly wary. I reached out with my long arm and caught his heavy tunic at the neck. "If I am only a woman, as you seem to believe, then why did you come after me with three?" I shook him. "It seems that you must have some regard for my skills, admitted or not." I lifted him entirely off the ground with one hand and drove the fist of the other against the side of his head. His foot lashed out, and I caught it and wrenched it, pulling the knee from its socket. He screamed.

I hung him in a tree, tucking a broken stub of branch beneath the tail of his tunic. I hung his sons beside him. They kicked and cursed, but I left them there, to escape or to be found at the whim of fate.

The sun was rising. I caught up my pack and my stick and set off along the muddy way. The brisk workout had set my blood singing. Suddenly, I felt enthusiasm for the new direction my life had taken.

The world opened out before me, and I moved forward into it.

WHO COURTS
A RELUCTANT MAIDEN

It had been a longish day. Though I had been walking the roads for weeks now, I still found it unsettling to have no place that could be called my own, no clean bed and, worst of all, no secure bathing place. The grit I had accumulated over the days since I had found my last secluded pool was becoming unbearable. My long shanks, too, were aching from their efforts.

When a thick wall loomed up above the young wood across my way, and I saw that it was topped with a modest tower, large enough to serve a keep of some size, I resolved to find work there for a few days. My store of silver was untouched, since I had bartered work for food and shelter along my way. But I had found that seeking honest work is different for a woman than for a man. Particularly a woman of my stature, homeliness, and shape. More than one woodcutter or small-holder had taken my unattached state to be an invitation. I had set them straight as gently as possible, but I feared that I had left some ruffled feathers in my path. The few nobles I had found in my way had treated me more courteously, once they learned my former station and present attitudes. There had been subtle hints, perhaps, but those I could avoid in good grace without damaging the pride of the hinter.

Now I was ready to rest, to wash well and in privacy, and to find something that suited my inches to earn my keep for a time. I rounded the curve of forest and faced a tall gate. A grubby youngster in a mail shirt met me there. He held a rusty pike and wore a helm with its crest shorn off. It came much too far down his forehead, so that he had to cock his head far back to see even so far as my shoulders. He was also barefooted, which spoiled his martial effect somewhat.

I stifled my smile and greeted him with sober respect. "Hail, Watchman. What hold is this, and who is its master?"

The young scamp leered at me. His lip curled lasciviously, as he peered up like a new-hatched chick from its unshed shell and said, "This is the keep of Kranold, held by the Lord Dorin, son of Anthell. None enters here without naming himself."

I had been looking at the wall above us as he answered, and a line of heads told me that the security of Kranold was not totally in the hands of such a fragile watchman. Glints of some bright metal showed that pikes and blades lived also upon the wall.

I looked down at the youngster. His tone had been uncivil, but I answered him politely, "Grittel Sundotha, daughter of the Master of Sundoth, to the south. I seek honest work for a day or a week, while I rest from the road."

He lowered his pikestaff's butt to the ground and brought its shaft up and out of my way. "Enter, then. You will find that there is always . . . work . . . for a female in the walls of Kranold." There was something in his voice that roused wariness all through me. If I had been less weary, or smaller, I would have gone down the road again. As it was, I gripped my knobstick tightly as I marched through the gate and into the dirty enclosure beyond it.

Kranold swarmed with brats and dogs and poultry. Slatternly women splashed in a fountain at the other side of the courtyard while slovenly men lounged about and watched them, making lewd remarks. Horse-droppings and slops made the footing treacherous, and I picked my way to the side of a middle-aged woman who seemed to have taken herself as far from her companions as possible. When she looked up at my greeting, I could see in her eyes such misery of spirit that I forgot my errand.

"Lady," I said, "I would gladly help you, if I might. What is your sorrow?"

She looked at me sidewise. While she considered, I ducked my head under the cool water and came up sputtering and scrubbing. As I smoothed back my wet braids, I found that her gaze was fixed upon my face. There was the trace of a smile on her lips, but her pale eyes held a faint hint of spirit.

Glancing about to see who might be nearby, she wrung

the last of the garments that sogged at her elbow. Then she gestured for me to follow her and set off across the court. I hurried after her.

She did not go directly across the courtyard after all. She slipped quietly into an alleyway that led to a street beyond a bulk of stone buildings. Her door opened into a room so narrow that it was the merest cranny. When that door was firmly shut and barred behind us, she motioned for me to sit upon her narrow cot, while she took the low stool that was the only other furnishing. In those close confines, our heads were only inches apart. Still she lowered her voice to a whisper.

"Daughter, this is a place of peril! Flee it as soon as the gates open tomorrow. Here stands a den of wickedness past any that the story-mongers ever dreamed of. The Lord, Dorin Anthelles, is served not only by the worst of men but also by a demon. He is a man of such insatiable lusts that fully half of those you saw about the fountain were stolen away from their proper places to serve him. Most of the brats in the streets are of his get, and he urges them to small wickednesses for his amusement. His wife is locked away in the tower beyond the court. She is quite mad, they say, from his cruelties and his sorceries. No female is safe, if he can set eyes upon her. Your unusual stature would make you a prize, to his warped thinking."

I took her hand. "You were stolen so?" I breathed. "Your face holds pain."

Her breath was rough in her throat as she answered, "He took me from the side of my husband, as we worked our own fields. My man fought to save me, but we had only farming tools. The ragtag villains who follow Dorin killed him before my eyes, and I was dragged away and racked until I complied with that evil man's wishes. He tired of me soon enough, but he never frees any whom he has taken. What became of my child, who had been left at home with a fever, I do not know. No word as ever come to me about her, though I question every traveler I can meet."

"You will go out with me tomorrow, as I leave," I said firmly. "I do not leave anyone to such a dismal life as yours must be."

"You do not know Dorin. His demon guards, even when his men sleep. It may be that you will not be let to go . . . and this is a place of torture and terror for those who refuse him what he wants. Hurry away from Kranold!"

Now I am fairly peaceable most of the time. I have, however, a flaw in my character that used to set my mother wild. Injustice heats my blood to boiling. I long to thrash those who practice it. Indeed, there are those in my father's hold who have felt the weight of my fist merely for beating their wives or children. Now the woman's tale roused the anger that usually lies dozing inside me.

Yet I recalled something from my travels that might comfort this poor woman. "Did you live near a swamp to the east of the southward road?" I asked her.

Her pale eyes lit with intense interest. "Aye. In a small house with a sod roof, set beneath a big arrel tree."

I nodded. "I was benighted near there. There were those upon the road whom I avoided, but I feared to enter the swamp by night. I asked shelter at that very house. A lady so old that her sharp chin near thrust holes in her knees lived there with a young girl of twelve or so. She called the child Seerah. Her name was Loe. Is it possible that the child was yours?"

She sighed. It was as if that gust of air bore out of her all the long years of torment and worry, for when she looked at me again her face was clear and strong.

"That woman is my husband's granddam. Seerah is my child. For this word, I will serve you in any way I can. They were quite whole and well?"

"Entirely. Strong and able, too, for they told me that the two of them grow enough in the fields to feed themselves and a bit more. They want for nothing necessary. One who watched from the shelter of the swamp saw what happened to you and your man. He cared for the child and sent word to her relatives."

She leaned forward, in her turn. "Rianna Telatha owes you a great debt. And you are, yourself, in much danger at this moment, for that saucy wretch at the gate reports all who come to his master. You must beware the demon. It lives in Dorin's house, sits by his table at meals, watching, watching. Those who have defied him in its presence are frozen by its gaze, and sometimes they fall dead. For that reason he never takes it into his torture chamber. He enjoys burning and racking his victims. He wants to lose none of them to death.

"The demon is called Jereel . . . but that is not its name. For lack of any better plan, I set myself to learn its true one. I have listened beneath windows, crept through alleys and attics for many years to find that valuable name. Its name is Azatoth. Do not forget that, for it may be useful to you before you win free of Kranold."

At that moment there came a rapping at the door. No polite request for entry, indeed, but an arrogant thumping that set my volatile blood singing in my veins. When my companion loosed the latch, the door flew back to slam against the wall. A hulking creature stood there with a whip in his dirty hand.

"Word from the Master," he drawled, looking me up and down. A smirk warped his grimed face. "He invites Grittel Sundotha to dine with him. The sun is near down, and food is ready. He says that he knows of your father and wishes to honor his daughter."

I heard a hiss behind me, and I knew what sort of honor I might expect from the Master of Kranold. But I set a good face upon it, taking up my pack and bidding my hostess farewell. As I settled the pack on my back, I felt a fumbling at my boot. Something long and thin slid down beside my shank, and I knew that the lady had supplied me with a blade—a princely gift that she must have stolen in her pryings about the city.

Dorin Anthelles was a red-beard of good height. Though he had been, I could see, a formidable man in the near past, soft living and overindulgence had dulled the edge of his wit and his strength. He had a bulge at his belly and pads of flesh on his face, surrounding his sharp blue eyes with puffy skin. He would have towered over any ordinary woman and most men, but he was forced to look up at me. A fact that did not lie well in his mind, as I could see.

He met me at the door of the inner keep and insisted upon taking my pack and setting it beside the door. "It is seldom that one of good blood comes passing by upon the road . . . and even more seldom that it is one of the fair sex," he rumbled, as his housekeeper set warm water before me for washing.

As he spoke, I met her eye. That dark organ sparked a warning that was gone as soon as perceived. I smiled. "I should think that even less often than that do you entertain a lady of my inches," I said, emphasizing the word lady.

He looked up at me as we went into the chamber where the meal was laid. In his eyes was the look that angered me most of all. He saw me as a challenge, as if I were a wild horse to be broken to the bit. But I smiled and sat and ate and made senseless conversation.

When the meal was done, he gestured toward the door of an adjoining room. I tensed, for I suspected what was coming, and I had no wish to see more of him or his grim and stony house. Yet I maintained my composure, saying, "It grows late, Lord Dorin. I must be early upon the road tomorrow. My thanks for your hospitality. I must return to the house of my friend and rest." As I spoke, I felt a chill creep over me. Looking about as unobtrusively as I could, I found myself looking into the red eyes of Dorin's demon. It was sitting on a ledge above the doorway toward which he had gestured.

It was the ugliest of creatures, snouted and horned

and greasy-gray, but I looked into its eyes defiantly. I thought its name, AZATOTH, at it. It shifted uneasily.

Dorin laughed aloud. "Little rest need you look for tonight, Grittel Sundotha. You have at last found a man to match your inches. Come now, and I'll warrant you'll not willingly leave me tomorrow."

I sighed. "I dislike discourtesy, sir, but I must decline. I intend to remain a maid until I meet one who touches my heart."

The demon curled its barbed tail and rose on its haunches. I sent, once again, a barb of thought toward it. *Azatoth!* It disappeared in a curl of smoke. I devoutly hoped that my knowledge of its name would send it sulking for a goodly time.

Dorin was staring upward, startled at the disappearance of his demon. Then he jerked his head, and I felt a touch upon my shoulder. The filthy one with the whip caught me and stood ready to hold me for his master. I slammed backward with my elbow, bringing him forward, doubled over, and clubbed him behind the head with a fist. He went flat.

Dorin's eyes widened, then narrowed. He whistled, and all those verminous men who walked the walls and lounged about the courtyard poured into the room. Before I could stir, I was caught by many hands and held immobile.

"You might have been gently treated," he said, though his eyes belied his words. "Now you must be persuaded, and that is always a long affair." His gaze was gleeful.

In moments, I had been hung by my wrists and ankles,

spread-eagled upon the wall of his torture chamber, which he had placed conveniently in a windowless scullery near his bedchamber. His rule, depending as it did upon terror, could only be strengthened by the screams of his victims. But the scullery had not been built in the solid manner of a true dungeon. As I flexed my forearm, the bolts moved slightly in the old mortar of the wall. I settled back, reassured. To one of my strength, the pulling-out of bolts is no major task. I felt sure that one like Dorin would never think that any maid, however large, might accomplish that.

I waited in the dim light of dripping torches. There was moaning and talk, just out of my sight in the next room. I guessed that Dorin and his men were bringing the executioner to his scanty senses. Then there was the sound of feet approaching, the clunk of a heavy door settling into place, and the rattle of bolts. That was good. The many who waited outside might otherwise have posed a problem.

Two sets of boots came toward me. Dorin came into view, followed by the whip handler. I flexed my arm again, and the bolt moved even more readily than before. The other arm moved also, though I hid my efforts from those who were coming.

Dorin signaled. The big fellow drew back his whip. I jerked my wrist sharply. The right hand came free, then the left, and I caught the whip as it fell. I jerked, and the big executioner stumbled forward as I kicked loose my feet and stepped away from the wall. His head hit the stone with a satisfying crunch. I stamped, hard, on the back of his neck. It broke with a loud snap.

Dorin stepped back, his eyes wary in a suddenly-pale

face. "Jereel!" he called. His hand fumbled with his sword-hilt, but I gave him no time to draw the blade. The weapon that Rianna had slipped into my boot was now in my hand. I spun on one heel, knocking his legs from under him with my booted foot. Then I was upon him, the thin metal of Rianna's blade against his throat. I pulled him backward by the hair and smiled into his wild blue eyes.

I could feel the gaze of the demon on my back, as I half-lifted the sagging hulk and towed him toward the wall. That being another problem entirely, I ignored it, hoping that the thing would be puzzled as to what it should do. I fastened Dorin securely into the set of shackles next to those I had torn out.

"Your hospitality is not of the best, Master of Kranold," I said. "I find it rude and graceless. Almost as much so, indeed, as yourself. It occurs to me that you have entertained many in this place, but you have not tasted its fare for yourself. I intend to remedy that, Dorin Anthelles."

I shackled him, spread-eagled, facing toward the wall. Now I could see the muscles quiver in his shoulders, as I ripped away his tunic and pantaloons. He struggled, but he could not rival my feat with the bolts. When the first lash of the whip curled across his skin, he screamed frantically. I could hear voices and shufflings at the door he had bolted, but I paid no heed to them. Or, indeed, to the demon that I could not see, but whose presence I felt. I proceeded to whip that lecher skinless. I have flayed game that looked less raw. His shrieks punctuated the cracks of the whip. I savored every one of them, thinking of the abused women and ill-reared children who were even now listening to those cries.

When my arm grew tired, I inspected my handiwork. The dried blood that had coated the floor was refreshed with that of the man who had put it there. I felt there were many in the hold of Kranold who would rejoice in secret that its master had been served so.

Then I turned to face the demon. As I looked about for it, it wisped into view atop the rack that stood against the wall. Those red eyes were filled with angry fires, but there was unease there also. It glared at me, and I felt that chill at my spine again. I planted my booted feet and stared into those evil eyes.

"*Azatoth!*" I cried aloud. "I have whipped your master to the bone. I will not fear you, who are his servant and creation. Get you down upon your belly! I will fear no demon, however ill and ugly."

The thing's eyes sent their deadly beams toward me, and I stood to face them. If I were to die here and now, I would count my life well spent. I refused to fear death, or any wicked thing made by cruelty. "Do your worst!" I cried.

A strange burning chill wrapped me round. I stiffened myself against it, pulling my spirit away into the deep place where it has always taken refuge at need. My hand loosed, and the blade fell to the floor with a clang. Teeth chattering in a purely physical reaction, I waited upon fate to decide the outcome.

The thing on the rack seemed to waver. Its shape grew

thin, then thinner. Only the red eyes now glowed at me. I still stood, against its will. And in that moment I understood a powerful thing . . . it is the demon you fear that can do you harm. As I thought that, it disappeared completely.

Chilled to the bone, I bent and retrieved my weapon. Then I looked about for Dorin's and took it into my right hand. Approaching the door, I listened for a moment. Then I loosed the bolts and stepped back to let the rush of men past.

When they turned to find me waiting to dally with anyone who wished to play, they looked at my blades and declined. I motioned them back, went through the door, and bolted it from the other side, thus penning up the entire guard of Kranold.

Dorin's housekeeper was an imperturbable lady. When I called for water to wash in, she brought it quietly, along with food and a good cloak of light wool, never saying a word. She looked neither glad nor sorry. But I caught that glint deep in her eyes, and I felt that Dorin would find himself without her when he freed himself. She nodded as I left.

I went at once to Rianna's door and rapped. She opened quickly, and I handed her the blade that had served me so well, saying, "You are free to go to your child. The guard is pent up with the master in the inner keep. I am about to deal with the watch." As I swung up the way, I heard the pat of her feet behind me.

The gate was securely barred, staves of metal being driven through the hasps of its leaves. It was no terrible task to loose them, but the watch came yawning from his post as I opened the gates.

This was another rude youngster, much like the other. He presumed to try to stop me, and I rapped him on his helmed skull with my fist. He sat flat on the ground. Then I shouted with all my strength, "Any who want to go free may do it now!" I lifted the groggy youth, remembering Arek and his two, and thrust his pike into the ground before the gateway. I stuck him onto it, running the shaft between his belted tunic and his skin. As I walked away, I could hear him shouting threats and curses and thumping his feet against the pikestaff.

I grinned at the white-starred sky. Once more, I set my feet into the road.

GRITTELLIA,
SORCERESS

I hefted my knobstick and found my balance as they came at me, one from each side and the third from the back. Though I could not see that one, I could feel his rush, and I spun on my heel, cracking three insufficiently-protected skulls with a satisfying: Thick! Thack! Thock!

They lay in the dust of the road, their eyeballs rolled back into their heads. I took time to look them over, but none were wearing any insignia of service. I could think of only one of the lords I had encountered so far in my journeying who might have reason to object to my continued existence, and there was nothing about these three to connect them with him. They seemed to be a mere taggle of cutthroats, looking for any coin I might carry and a moment's cruel pleasure. I took their blades (obviously stolen, for they were of worked metal, rare as that may be), their sharpened staves, and their jerkin-braces. Then I walked away, leaving them to come to their senses as they would.

As I ambled away down the road, I forgot them. They might follow or not as they liked. Three of their kind were no match for me. As I went, I mused sadly upon the inconveniences of life on the road. But I could not regret refusing the match my mother had made, no matter what the consequences had been. I wondered if my sisters had acquired suitors since my departure from our home. I hoped that they had; that would take them away from Mother's adder tongue, if nothing else.

I sighed. No man had ever looked upon me with affection. Since my leave-taking, a woman or two had made advances, but those I took across my knee and made their bottoms blush like roses.

As a matter of fact, I have found that folk approach me in one of three ways: As an oddly-shaped man; as a repulsive and somehow frightening freak; or as a challenge to be broken and ground into the dirt. The first I can bear. The second I can at least understand. The third fills me with anger and disgust. Common or noble, few have regarded me simply as a person, like to themselves in my heart, if not in my frame.

Now the light was beginning to fade from the sky. I had left the wooded lands for cleared fields, and they were gray with twilight on either hand. Beyond them the great forest that wraps this land in an almost unbroken cloak to the edges of the uplands stood, dark and silent. I looked far ahead up the narrow track. Cow dung and cart-tracks told me that a farmstead must be close ahead, so I did not make off across the fields to find the haven of some well-branched tree for the night.

Instead, I hurried through the gathering darkness, seeing with relief a light kindled far ahead, marking out the shape of a narrow window. As I drew near, I smelled kine and heard their soft breathing from the byre beside the lane. A dog began to bark, and a door opened, letting out a reddish fan of pitchlight.

A stocky figure stood in the doorway, his staff in his hands, and by his stance I knew that he understood its uses.

"Greeting," I called. "A traveler begs shelter for the night, in return, perhaps, for a day's labor tomorrow."

My voice belies my looks. It is quiet and not too deep. It reassured him, for he stepped out and said, "What is a woman doing upon this perilous road, so late and alone?"

By now I was almost to the circle of light on the lane. I paused and said, "A rather strange woman, though not unfriendly to those who do me no harm. You may be astonished by my height." I stepped forward so that he could see me.

His eyes traveled up and up to find my face. Then they traveled down again. Men, whatever their age, invariably do this. But he was a seemly old fellow and made no great show of it. Then he gestured toward the house and called to his wife to bring bread and cheese for me, their own meal being long over.

They were somewhat past middle life. He was square as his own byre, with a crown of grizzled hair that stood up about a massive bald place atop his head. His bright blue eyes were cheery. They were also wary, though he was full of the good manners that I had found in every self-respecting farmer.

She was a wisp of gray gown, gray hair, gray eyes, gray manner. When she did not move, she was invisible. I liked them both at once.

"I am Grittel," I told them. "Daughter to the Master of Sundoth, far to the south. As you can see, I am no daughter to grace a hold in idleness and fair seeming, and my mother sent me forth when I refused the match she made. Though I will say that my father would willingly have kept me at work in his fields."

The woman's gray eyes peered up at me. "We are Adona and Mikkels. Our own younglings are grown and gone about their ways . . . those who yet live. We tend our small fields and our cattle. With the bounty of the forest, that makes enough for us. No lord claims this place, for it is too distant from any hold, little worth seizing. We are not rich but . . ." Here she looked at me with something like pity in her eyes. ". . . we have had the long comfort of our marriage. That is no small wealth."

I saw that she was, in her awkward way, feeling her way toward an understanding of what it must be like to be one who might well never find one with whom to make a life. I was not irritated by her words, but smiled down and said, "Tomorrow I might try doing some of the more difficult tasks, to repay you for sheltering me. Winter is not far away, and it is well to be prepared beforehand."

Mikkels rose from the bench beside his hearth and stretched. "Our thanks, Grittel Sundotha. Now eat and stretch yourself . . ." He looked about to find a spot long enough to accommodate my length. ". . . before the doorway. I shall lay a tanned hide to ease the chill of the draught."

Their day would have ended long before this, I knew, if I had not arrived. I made haste to eat and to unroll my blankets on the hide that he put down for me. They retired at once to their cupboard bed, which had been set into the wall beside the fireplace, and pulled the wooden doors tightly shut. The thought of trying to sleep imprisoned so, breathing the stifling fug that must be its atmosphere, made my chilly pallet feel almost luxurious.

It had been a long day. I had tramped more than twenty miles, thrashed three ruffians, and made two friends. Feeling that I had earned my rest, I drifted into sleep with a good conscience. However, the third eye that my months of rough living had waked in me kept its usual watch over the surroundings.

Hours later I woke. In the same instant I was on my feet and into my boots. A stir in the byre . . . shiftings and snorts and uneasy grunts among the cattle . . . spoke of intruders there. A tiny click told me that the gate-latch had been lifted. A slight fumbling at the door sent me back to tap lightly at Mikkels's cupboard. While he woke, I took the blade I had won from Dorin from my pack, looked at it, then laid it aside in favor of my knobstick.

Mikkels had lived for long on the fringes of civilization. He came forth silently, his staff in his hand, evidently brought from some recess in the cubby. Adona followed. The glimmer of the few coals left in the fireplace glinted on a narrow blade in her hand.

I put my mouth to his ear and breathed, "He . . . or they . . . will think you to be only two, perhaps. Is there a way that I can go out and take them from the rear when they break in the door?"

Mikkels didn't answer, but I felt his head nod. He took my hand and led me to the back corner of the house, where the roof came within inches of the top of my head. He raised his hands. In the dim light I saw him make a lifting motion. Following his direction, I lifted against the roof. The square section just above me moved, thatch and all, quietly upward.

I stuck the blade into the loop of my belt, thrust my knobstick up to hold the opening, then pulled myself up and through. Standing on the strawstack just beside the wall, I replaced the section of roof and moved to peer around the corner of the hut that was near on my left. Standing there, listening intently, I wondered if the dog that had warned of my coming now lay dead before the door. There was no sound from it, and now even the kine had settled again to rest.

Only the clumsy fumbling and muttering at the door were to be heard. Guided by that, I made my way along the side of the house until I reached the low fence that divided its vegetable patch from the road. Stepping over it, I was brought up short by a husky whisper.

"They'm got a stout bar across that door, Gwim. We'm got to force 'un, do we get in at all."

Another whisper answered. "Get a log from the stack. We'll break it in. These old farmers always have a gold coin or two hidden away behind a chimney-stone. And if that big beast of a woman has sheltered here, we'll have a bit of sport, too." That voice was cold, with a hint of culture. Another "noble," I had no doubt. A younger son gone bad, perhaps, and fallen to preying upon those who should have been his responsibility.

I let them grope about, finding their log and getting it into position. Added to my original three were two more. Four of them grasped the battering ram, the fifth, Gwim, no doubt, standing aside to oversee the proceedings. As they started their run toward the door, I burst around the corner of the hut, shouting, my stick a wheel of spinning wood.

The errant noble went down first. I found time to hope that this was a second dose of the knobstick for him. Then I was among the demoralized door-bashers. They promptly dropped their log. From the immediate screams and moans, I assumed that the log chosen had been sizeable and that it had fallen upon several sets of toes or shins.

For the first time in my life, a war-cry rose in my throat. I let it rip free. "Grittellia Floresca!" I found it far more suitable for a war-cry than for a name.

Behind me, the door opened. Stout Mikkels came forth, and I could hear the swish-thunk! of his staff, even above the noisy activity of my own. My blade was unneeded. Of the four who had been left in possession of their senses, two had been rendered temporarily unfit by the falling of the log. The other two went down as readily as grain before the scythe, one to me, the other to Mikkels.

Then Adona came running out with one of the pitch-knots that served as their light. The four ruffians we bound securely and dragged into the wood-house to pass the rest of the night. Gwim, who wore the ragged remnants of good leather mail and a pair of splendid new boots (obviously recently stolen from some victim), we took into the hut. I wanted to reason with him. Or some such.

"What will we do with these?" asked Adona, always practical, as her man and I set the now-groaning Gwim against the bench by the hearth. "They'll come back and burn us out, do we loose them. We canna kill them. 'Twould be an unholy act, with them all undone."

"I think that they followed me to you," I told the pair. "I had an . . . encounter . . . with them earlier in the day. I feel it is only just that I take them away again. Let me question this creature a bit. Then I'll think on what can be done. Worry no more . . . in one way or another I will see them well away from you and yours."

They settled again in their cupboard, leaving me sitting in the renewed firelight with our captive. I added enough fuel to make a good blaze. Then I sat and watched Gwim come to his senses. He took his time about it, but eventually his eyes opened and focused upon the fire, then on me. They widened, and he struggled to free his hands.

I grinned at him. He blanched and looked down at the thongs that held him fast. His mouth twisted angrily, but his hands and feet could not move. He spat a few choice epithets in my direction.

I laughed. "The boot is firmly upon the other foot, Gwim," I told him. "No golden coins, no evening of lust and torture will you find here. Unless, of course, you really do desire torture? I could probably oblige you, if you insist."

His eyes flicked frantically to right and left, but I said, "You need not look for your henchmen. They are bound even more securely than you and stacked like cordwood in the shed. No, we are quite alone here. And there are some questions to which I sincerely hope that you will supply answers. Such as your motive for attacking me, this morning? I hardly think my beauty overcame you. When I searched you, I found far more silver than a small thief of your kind should have, even on a good day. It smacked of blood money. If you understand my meaning?"

I paused. He spat in my direction. Sadly, I took the blade that I had leaned against the hearthstones and used it to push the metal rod I had found by the fireplace until its end rested among the reddest of the coals.

"Secondly," I continued, "what family has stricken your name from its records? You were once well-reared and gently taught. I would like to know whom to notify, when all our business is done."

The poker had begun to glow redly. I wrapped its handle in a rag and drew it forth, spat on it, then set it back, still sizzling.

"Thirdly, from what larger band have you detached yourselves? You are not of the ilk that could, or would, make your way so independently. Your sort runs in packs far larger than a mere hand's count."

His eyes were now set upon the red-white tip of the rod. His throat worked as I took it again into my hand, nudging a few straggling coals into the fire. I smiled at him and reached out, drawing off one of his fine boots with one pull.

"You will answer," I said. "If not just now, then later. You have the choice." The poker glowed at the tip, and his gaze followed its bright pattern in the dim room.

I sighed as he remained mute. Setting my big leg across his bared shin and ankle, I brought the red-hot rod toward his cringing toes.

You must understand that I am something of a chicken-heart, when I am not angry. I made sure that he could see nothing of what I did, for the bulk of my leg and knee hid his own feet from him. I touched the heel of my own boot with the poker, simultaneously touching his bared foot with the blade in my other hand.

He screamed with expected and imagined pain. I looked up. "Ah, you are ready?" I asked, holding the rod as if for another pass at his foot.

"Gwim an-Harrath," he choked, tears running from his tightly closed eyes. "Last son of twelve. Beaten and tormented and driven from home by my elders before I was fifteen."

"That is a fine beginning," I said, laying the rod back into the fire. "And I feel for you. I know what it is to be a misfit in my family. Now tell me who set you on my track."

"Dorin . . . Dorin Anthelles, whose hold you passed before midsummer."

Ah. "Dorin of the red beard and the winning manner? I recall him well. He thought to hang me upon his dungeon wall until I consented to all that he wished of me. I cracked his whipmaster's neck and took his whip to the Master of Kranold. Has his skin grown again, or is he still striped from head to heel?"

"One stroke of the lash," whispered the unhappy Gwim, still refusing to open his eyes, "castrated him. He will never forgive that."

Then I laughed long and hard. In that foul hold had been many women, torn from their homes and those they loved, to serve his whims. None had seemed still whole, in mind or in body. His bastards numbered one for one with the poultry in the filthy courtyard. No fate more fitting had ever been bestowed upon a cruel lecher. And that had been done without intent. I had whipped him. The gods had seen to the rest.

I sobered a bit and asked, "Your companions . . . where are they? How many?"

"Garbat's band is ours. They were making northward when we fell in with Dorin. They will wait for us at Four-Ways Well. They will expect a share in our payment." He almost opened his eyes . . . but he evidently thought that his inability to see his wounded foot must be the reason that he wasn't feeling the effects of the burning. He kept them closed.

"You have done well, if unwillingly. Now lean your head against the wall. Think of darkness . . . darkness . . . darkness . . . and I will heal your toes so that you will never know that they were touched," I said soothingly. "I have many powers. This is not the least useful of them." I almost giggled at the terrible lie, but he was ready to believe anything just then.

His head dropped back. I blew gently against his naked toes.

"Now," I said. "Open your eyes."

His amazement almost sent me into a fit of laughing that would have betrayed the trick, but I managed to keep a straight face as he surveyed his unmarked skin. When he looked at me, I could see fear, too, in his eyes. From that moment, I well knew, Garbat's band would carry tales of a giant wizardess abroad to all the land. It suited me quite well.

So it was that I set off the next morning accompanied by five subdued and fearful villains. Adona and Mikkels, being very shrewd and having listened with amusement to my midnight talk with Gwim, understood the situation quite well. I could see laughter struggling behind Mikkels's bright blue eyes and even Adona seemed a bit more substantial as she reached up to place a wispy kiss upon my cheek.

"Luck go with you," she said, as I herded my charges before me, setting out northward toward Four-Ways Well.

To my relief, the dog had been found alive, though stunned, and it panted along at my side for a half-league, before giving me a tongue-lolling smile and setting out for home. Then I drove my captives at a rapid pace. We hastened through fields and forests, past lonely huts and untenanted reaches for three days. All five began to look gaunt and weary.

At night I didn't trouble to bind them very tightly. They fell into sleep almost before finishing their food, and only my boot waked them again to go on in the morning.

When at last Gwim gasped, "The well is an hour's journey ahead," I nodded with satisfaction.

"I am returning to you most of your pay," I said. "Some of it I keep for my trouble." (I had actually given it to Mikkels, but I wanted no backward glance turned that way.) "But the rest you may share out as you please. Yet listen closely to my words. Make no southward journeys. Pay no more visits to the hut where I caught you. I will know, if you do, and I will leave no scrap attached to any other. Believe me!"

Gwin did believe. His terror convinced the other four as no word of mine might have done. Satisfied, I watched them out of sight.

Then I turned my face eastward, where a game trail intersected the road. For a time, I thought, it might be as well to walk unpeopled ways and to think on the habits of mankind from a distance. I wanted no curious band at my heels, seeking to learn the ways of wizards. I hefted my knobstick and whirled it about my head. Then I slid into the shelter of the forest, leaving no track upon the springy mold underfoot.

IV

THE WITCH DOWN THE WOOD PATH

The forest stretched away on either hand. For two days I had walked through the reaches it covered without trouble, but now its character had changed. Except for the path I trod, it seemed unmarked in this place. As if even beasts shunned it. No bird called from the thickets. Not even a beetle scuttered underfoot.

Though I had thought to find solitude in the wood, this was entirely too silent to suit me. A wood should be alive with tiny sounds in the leafy mold, the chacking of throstles in the trees, and the soft movements of small creatures among the berry bushes. Still, I had no mind to turn back, for I did not intend to court the company of any of Garbat's band, or their like. I shrugged my pack to a more comfortable position, gripped my knobstick, and went cautiously.

Past the thick undergrowth that bordered this area, I

found myself in old forest, whose gnarled oaks and soaring ash trees made a distant roof above the dim path. The light was almost a twilight, though it was well before noon. I found myself peering closely to find the marking of the winding track in the mulch of the forest floor. After walking for an hour or so, I raised my eyes again to take my bearings.

For the first time in my wanderings, I found myself completely turned about. There was no sky visible so that the sun might be a guide. The path had looped so intricately that I had lost all sense of direction, and the light had become so very dim that I couldn't retrace its windings and go back as I had come. I was lost. It had become impossible even to follow the trail forward.

As I stood, bemused, there came a sound, at last, into the wood. A cackle of shrill laughter echoed about me, though I could see nobody in the darkness of the wood.

I shivered all down my great length. The laughter grew louder. "Does Grittel, the great warrior-sorceress, the seven-foot maiden of uncertain temper, the disobedient daughter . . . does even she find my forest a bit frightening?" teased the voice.

"If you know so much, you know that I am no sorceress at all and only a warrior when necessity drives," I said, as calmly as I could manage. "Who are you? Where are you?"

There was no answer for a moment. Then, as I felt my senses beginning to spin lazily, as a twig spins in the grip of an eddy in a stream, I heard it again. Softly it spoke into my ear. "You did not fear the demon. You faced it down in the place of its making. Do not think to deceive me." As the darkness about me crept into my mind, I realized that this was true enchantment. I held onto myself with all my strength, but the world slid sideways, and blackness dropped over me like a bag of darkness.

I didn't want to awaken. My senses kept niggling at me, and for a long while I kept pushing them back down into the mist of unconsciousness. Yet at last I slitted my eyes, unable to deceive myself into the comfort of unconsciousness any longer.

I hung upon a wall. Manacles held my wrists above my head, though not at full stretch, which was a mercy. I had been hung on a wall before, and to be fully extended grows old very quickly indeed. My feet were bound together, the toes just able to reach the floor. This told me something valuable. My captor might be an enchanter of much skill, but she (I was almost sure it was a she) was ignorant of the correct method of securing a prisoner to the wall. In my short career since leaving home, I had acquired some experience in that art, from both sides of the question.

I sighed. I may be homely. I may, indeed, be short-tempered and intractable. But I do have one talent: I can get into more predicaments than anyone I ever heard of. And I was in another right now. I looked about the room in which I was confined.

It was not large enough to be a chamber in a keep. Still neither was it small enough to be a peasant's cottage.

About ten paces across and half that in width, it was walled with what looked to be mud and floored with dampish stone. A very smoky fire cast a wavering light over everything, though I could see through the one narrow window on the wall opposite me that it was still day. The darkness in the wood must have been a part of the spell that had trapped me.

The fittings of the room were not reassuring. Cages along the end wall held dejected badgers and foxes and weasels and parthions. A metal frame stood before the fireplace. There were manacles secured to it in odd locations. A huge mortar with a pestle the length of my arm stood against the other wall, surrounded by bags and baskets and bowls of anonymous dried stuff from which rose a strange medley of fragrances and stenches.

The skull on a low table was evidently used as a pen-holder, for a quill was thrust into one of the eye-sockets. A moldy old book lay on the table, too, and I could tell from the edges of the pages that it had been much used. A spell-book? Most likely.

Before I had finished my survey of the room, there was a step that gritted on the stone floor. A door opened in the wall at my back, but far down at the other end of the chamber. The ugliest old woman one could possibly imagine came into the room and set down a bag that squirmed. It also whimpered with the voice of a child.

Anger rose in me like steam in a kettle. Unless my ears had lost their cunning, a small one was confined in that bag. And even though I had declined the honor of becoming stepmother to nine untaught hellions, I am partial to children. I had intended, until my height revealed itself as such an obstacle, to marry and have a houseful of my own.

Nevertheless, I said nothing and watched, keeping my eyes all but closed. The crone gave the bag a thump, and the whimpering died away. Then she painfully manhandled a big iron pot onto the crane, filled it with water from a barrel beneath the window, and swung it over the fire to boil. Handfuls, pinches, and dollops of the contents of the noisome containers along the wall added their indescribable odors to the already thick atmosphere of the room.

She stumped past me without a glance, which told me that I was supposed to be still under her spell. She approached the line of cages and surveyed her captives carefully. Now and again she took one from its prison and hefted it in her hand. At the end of the row she took the weasel in hand, nodded, and set it back in its cage. Then she turned back to her pot.

After stirring the mess within it, she sat down at her table and opened the spell-book, tracing the characters with one knobbly finger and mouthing the words as she read. With the other hand, she made gestures that were midway between comical and obscene. I, however, did not feel like laughing. Something really evil and dangerous was afoot, my bones assured me.

I gave a subdued groan, as though I were only now awakening. Then, opening my eyes, I looked about in feigned bewilderment and asked, "Dame, where is this place? Why am I chained?" in the sort of fluttery voice that most women use to prove their helplessness.

She grinned, showing the stumps of blackened teeth, and came to look at me. She breathed spitefully into my face, and that was a terrible torture, indeed. My skin shrank from the foul gust, and my hair threatened to curl to cinders on my head.

Backing away to judge the effect of her initial attack, she said, "Why, I am An-Perria. This is my wood, by gift of the old kings. This is my home and workshop. No one comes into the wood of An-Perria without invitation. There are dire penalties. So for that cause you are chained. Even though I inveigled you here, myself. The first rule of my wood is that there is no justice in it."

She busied herself about my feet, and I found that the double-cuffed manacle had had its chain lengthened so that I could set my heels on the floor. She reached up and pulled at a lever, lowering my arms to a level at which she could gather the chains into her hands.

"Now we'll take a wee walk over to the fire, my girl. I'll hook you up to my little contraption, and you can toast while I pop the baby into the pot and skin the weasel. When we get through, I'll have the gift of all your strength, your talent, and your beauty."

I opened my mouth to deny the possession of any beauty at all. Then I looked at her and closed it again. By contrast, I had to admit, I was a smashing lovely.

She thought, I daresay, that the remnants of the spell

still lingered in my mind, subduing my will to hers. That was an error on her part that I did nothing to correct. Obediently, I stepped, with tiny steps, away from the wall in response to her tug on the chains. Then I reached down and lifted her, squalling like a cat, in one hand while I broke the rusted manacles away from my ankles with the other.

I twisted her up in my grip as though she were a hank of wool, avoiding the slashes of her discolored claws. Pausing beside the frame, I considered. Then I shook my head.

It was tight work getting her into the pot. She was squirming and kicking and spouting long and intricate curses and spells, which made it a long job altogether. Once the lid of the pot rose off the floor and whacked me in the rump. I had to stop what I was doing and put the thing outside, struggling all the while with my skinny burden, before I could get back to business.

At last I thought of stuffing her in head first. After that it was easy, though the bubbles did rise in purple and green for a while after her head went under. Then I popped the retrieved lid onto the thing and let it boil. I am not tenderhearted with folk who cook babies.

The child itself I soon had out of the stifling bag. She was a tiny thing, though she was no infant. Her green eyes and red-gold hair were magically pretty in the ugly room, and she sat, quite self-contained, with no tendency to weep, now. She simply waited before the hearth and looked about her in wonder.

I reckoned her age at three or there about, but she was so thin and pale that she might well have been less than two. Still, she looked at me with eyes too knowing for her size, and without the terror one would have expected from one of her age.

At last she found courage to speak. "Be there something to eat?" she whispered. "I am on hunger, most dearly."

While I rummaged about, looking for something clean and wholesome enough to feed her, I asked, "What is your name, child, and who are your people?"

"They'm call me Sivrain," she said. "But they'm not here. They'm somewhere else, *not here*. She'm come *through* and catch me."

I thought for a while, as I concocted oatcakes from a small store of grain and set them to bake on a griddle I found by the hearth. Her look was not of any of our people. Her talk was strangely accented and phrased. Neither noble nor common, it had an alien ring to it altogether. I wondered whether An-Perria had been skilled enough at her arts to go through the walls of our world-space into some other faerie sort of dimension that might adjoin it. The broth of a babe from such a world might well have potent attributes.

As I turned the oatcakes, I heard the sound of a broom, sweeping. Looking over my shoulder, I saw that she had picked up the hag's besom and was neatly removing the litter that bestrewed the floor. The broom stood higher than she, but she was manipulating it merely by waggling her finger. When she was done, she pointed at the farther wall, and the broom swished over and came to rest against it.

"You are so thin, Sivrain," I said to her, setting a steaming cake before her on a clean shingle. "Are your people so very poor?"

"Ah, no!" she exclaimed. "It be such a long way, from there to here. She'm *hop*, for herself, but I'm go very, very long before I'm here. Get very much on hunger."

"Then you'd go back, if there were a way?"

"Yes. Much like to go back," she said, through a mouthful of crumbs.

It was a daring thought that had come to me. I went to the table and saw that a candle-stub lay among the litter on it. Lighting that, I opened the spell-book and began to read. It was interesting. It contained matters that were purest common sense. It touched upon things highly useful to people of many kinds. It dealt in depth with much that no sane person would touch. Much of it was impractical for one unversed in the lore, and more was bloodthirsty. But at last I found something that fitted my problem almost too exactly.

HOW TO RETURN AN OTHERLING was the heading of the page, carefully written in a hand that could not have been An-Perria's. That, in itself, was promising. But the next line decided me. "Boil one witch in a brew of hellebore, vervain, and rue."

I read on to the end, then bent over the pots and bags she had used when mixing her potful. More than luck was with us, for they bore the correct names, scrawled in charcoal on their containers. I could not have chanced sending Sivrain into some dimension where she did not belong, so I was grateful for the sense that I was acting under some sort of guidance.

Well enough. I waited until Sivrain was finished with her cake. Then I set her on the hearth in the position prescribed in the book, kissed her on the forehead, and said, "I believe that this will work, child. We'll soon know."

I dipped a quill in the stinking potful and drew two circles on her forehead, one on her breast, and one on the back of each hand. Stepping back, I opened the book and read the words on the yellowed page. I hoped that my pronunciation would be accurate enough for our purposes.

"Ahiyallah, simoora; ahiyallah ahnaya misi. Gefallorn!"

There was a flash of brilliant light. The fire flared high, then died to a glimmer. Where Sivrain had sat nothing remained. I felt afar with all my might. Nothing troubled my heart, nothing stirred foreboding in my mind. I felt certainty that she had gone home again, in all safety.

Unwilling to spend the night in such filth, I busied myself with turning out all the captive beasts. I searched every cranny for any other prisoners, and in so doing found my pack in a filthy bedchamber that was running alive with rodents and lice. The only object of interest in the entire house was the spell-book. And, of course, the store of herbs for completing the recipes in it. I found myself feeling some certainty that I could make use of the esoteric art, so

I stuffed the book into my pack and made a good bundle of every sort of dried herb in the pots and bags.

I set the house afire as I left. It kindled quickly, and I went away through the wood with its warm light at my back. The forest was now just a wood, no great and silent place of enchantment. I made good time along its ways, stopping only when the last glimmer of the burning house was lost among the trees. Then I stood for a long time in the clean, chill wind of Autumn, looking up at the stars.

"Good night, Sivrain," I whispered. "Fare you well on your long way."

Then I turned away, knowing that I would always wonder about that strange little wayfarer and her unknown world.

V

A spell in time

Winter is a bad time for wandering the ways. Though my boots were still fairly stout and my clothing relatively unworn, I hated snow like a cat. No matter how carefully you step, it will get into your boots and set your feet to freezing. And no matter how meticulously you choose your path, eventually you are going to fall.

I had left the wooded lands behind me before the first snow fell and was making my way across the downlands. They were cut frequently by deep gullies that grew into canyons that were almost valleys, they were so broad. No keep or even cottage had I seen for days when I began my cautious descent into one of these declivities. I had begun to realize the rashness of going into sparsely tenanted lands in winter; and when I fell I had time, in my rough descent, to feel something like panic, for it was late evening, and the night promised to be terribly cold. But then I saw, once my rolling came to a halt, that I had slipped on a cattle path that had made a treacherous path of ice beneath a light powdering of snow.

There had been no stopping on that steep slope, and I had bunched myself and tumbled amid an avalanche of snow to the bottom. I had managed to get my pack under me, else I would have been sorely bruised by the underlying rocks. Finally I had fetched up against a low obstruction, and I lay for a moment to get my breath.

Snow was melting down my neck. My breeches were soaked, and my long braids were soggy. It would take little time to freeze in this state, I knew. I shook myself free of the clinging whiteness as well as I could, took up my pack, and looked about.

The strip of lowland was very broad here, and I could see that the thing that had stopped my slide was a low stone wall, almost covered with snow. What is more, I could smell smoke, though a scrubby growth of trees blocked any view I might have had of the area. The wind was knifing down the cut, bringing with it that hopeful odor, so I turned my face into it and followed my nose.

There seemed to be a path beside the wall; my feet found it before my head realized it was there. Soon a converging path covered with droppings and tracks showed me where the cattle had passed on their way to their byre. I stepped forth even faster.

Now the sky held only a lemon-colored streak of light across the west. Only the snowlight helped me to avoid the multiple cowpats in my way; I was grateful when they turned aside into a walled yard, leaving the last of the way clear to the low-roofed house that now showed against the white-piled orchard behind it. Light showed around shutters that hinted at generous windows. The scent of smoke was joined by that of roasted meat.

I stopped at the gateposts, both because it was a courteous thing to do and also because a dog fully half as tall as I blocked my way. Its voice rose in one brief sound, neither yelp nor howl. At that sound, the lights went out, and I heard a door opening, very cautiously.

"How, Garry? What troubles the night?" whispered a gruff voice.

I stood straight and said, "Only a maid afoot, needing shelter from freezing, Sir. Grittel Sundotha, I, daughter to the Master of Sundoth, far to the south. Do not be alarmed at my inches. I am most peaceable to those who offer me no injury."

There was a scritch. A lightglass beamed toward me. I noted with professional approval that the voice now came from a distance to one side, as it spoke again.

"Come forward, Grittel Sundotha. I warn you, if you be bait in a trap, it will go hard with any who threaten my household."

I stepped forward slowly, my hands free of my knobstick, which I had thrust into its loops on my pack. The light blinded me, and the voice told me to enter the house, taking care not to stumble on the doorstone. It was well I was warned, for the slab thrust up a full half-yard from the path.

Warm darkness greeted me, and I stood just inside

the door, waiting for someone to make a light. The panel closed behind me, and I could hear bars being drawn across and bolts slipped home. Then two lamps, in opposite corners of the room, bloomed into light.

It was a big, square chamber, half kitchen, half sitting-room, much like those I had seen many times in my wanderings. The two women beside the lamps matched their home, being simply dressed, fair of face, with a certain ease of bearing that spoke of good stock and careful teaching. The man who stepped past me to look into my face was another matter.

He looked as if a bear had sired him and a she-wolf suckled him. Not that he seemed cruel or wild. His face, what could be seen amid the luxuriant curling beard and the matching flame of hair, was shrewd and open. His eyes, so pale that they seemed to be looking through wide spaces of sky, saw to the heart of matters, I guessed, with no trouble whatever.

"When Garry merely spoke, without attacking you, I knew that you were not one of our enemies," he said.

The older woman came forward and held out her hand. "Welcome to our hold, Grittel Sundotha. How came you to be in our valley in this terrible weather?"

I looked into her dark eyes and smiled. "As you can see, Lady, I am no beauty, and my size is ungainly. When I rejected the one offer of marriage that my mother could contrive for me, she set my inheritance into my hand and my feet into the road. My sisters have no need to be embarrassed by such a sibling as I. So I roam the ways, working where I can, helping those I can aid. It is my fortune that the inches that so distressed my mother have kept me safe from those who might have abused me.

"I am skilled at all work about a farm, and I am not unskilled with blade and knobstick. Circumstances have seen to my learning something of defense, and my long reach is a handy thing to have. So cautious is your welcome that I wonder if you have need of another strong hand about this hold."

The young woman had said nothing thus far. Now she turned her magnificent blue eyes toward the man. "Arnulf, it might be that we could use her services. If the Clyverrin raid our herds again this winter, it will go hard with us. Even such as she must have their uses." Her lip curled as she spoke, and I saw that she was one of those who consider me a joke of nature, and not in the best of taste.

I am not a patient person. Those who have tried to patronize me have received short shrift, and I had no intention of being insulted by some useless bit of fluff, however beautiful and well-born she might be.

"Lady, I am not here as beggar or supplicant. Simply, I ask for shelter for one night, as I am wet with snow and the evening is bitter. I have my own food, and I own my own blankets. I have made my way among those nobler than you and humbler. From none of them have I accepted scorn. I am as the gods made me, and you must be satisfied with that."

Arnulf chuckled deep in his throat. I saw her sapphire

gaze flash toward him in annoyance. But any reply she might have made was forestalled by the lady who was obviously her mother. She turned on the girl a look that stifled the words in her throat. Then she held out her hand, again, to me.

"None has ever come to this door in peace and been turned away," she said. "The House of Orwen was once a place of much coming and going, with mirth and fellowship to warm the winter days. Now there are few left in these parts, and we live in isolation. It is ignorance of social custom that you may thank for Isola's ill manners. I am Dortha, Lady of Orwen. Arnulf, who is now my right arm, came, even as you, on a winter night, needing shelter and treatment for wounds suffered at the hands of the Clyverrin."

I shrugged my pack from my shoulders and sank onto a low stool before the hearth. As I struggled to remove my wet boots I asked, "And who are the Clyverrin? Twice they have been named, both times in dire contexts. My roots are in the far south, and I have never heard of a family named so."

The Lady Dortha stooped to shift the blazing logs with a rod, but not even the warm light could conceal the paling of her cheeks. "They are not truly a family, we believe. To their door can be laid the fact that we alone keep our home and our ways in the downs, now. They have harried away or killed those who were our neighbors. In the days when Isola was a babe, my own man, Ossian of Orwen, was their victim. We found him in the far meadow with an oaken stave thrust through him. He lived long enough to name his murderer, who took ten cows along with Ossian's life.

"There are many of them. They have ways that are both fierce and strange. Yet there is even more that cannot be clearly defined. There were a dozen families within two days' travel, in the old days. They numbered many more than the Clyverrin, and they were tough people, determined and wary. We tried to unite with them against those dangerous foes, but odd things happened to them. Some were stricken by lightnings. Others fell prey to direwolves, though such had not roamed here in any numbers for ages. Some simply did not return from their fields and pastures, and their bodies could not be found. There is power among the Clyverrin that draws to their hold the blackhearted and preys upon the upright. We alone have held onto our lands and our lives, here in Orwen Deep, and that would not have been true without Arnulf's skill and determination. Isola and I would have been taken away, long since, to serve the dark folk at Clyverrin, without his aid."

"A family of warlocks?" I asked, directing my question toward Arnulf.

"So it seems. Practitioners of black usages, it seems certain. And now that winter brings long nights, our danger is increased. We must fasten up our kine in the byre, else they would dwindle away in numbers. The direwolves howl beneath our windows when the snow lies over the land, and only the stout stone of Orwen holds out the things that threaten us.

"Skill at arms may be a useful thing against fully

human foes, but against these I have found that I must use wit and wile. There are traps on every path save that guarded by Garry. You are fortunate that your way lay as it did, for many of those traps are fatal to whatever falls into them."

I yawned, my eyes suddenly grown too heavy to hold open. "Tomorrow, I may have a suggestion, for I have had some experience with sorcerous lore. But now I am too weary to think. May I lay my blankets in yonder corner and rest?"

"Not in the corner, indeed. Abovestairs, in a clean bed with good woolens to pull about your ears. How long has it been, child, since you slept so?" the Lady Dortha asked.

"Entirely too long, indeed," I answered her. She caught up a pitcher and filled it with warm water from the kettle at the edge of the hearth. "And longer yet for washing. My thanks, Lady. Tomorrow, I hope that I may make some return for your kindness."

But as we left the chamber, I saw Isola's expression. That young woman was most annoyed, and Arnulf was watching her apprehensively. She would, I felt sure, be a most unpleasant housemate, when her temper was ill. And what a pity it was that she could not—or would not—see what I saw in the big man's eyes, when he looked at her. Perhaps she thought herself too fine for him. Or was it that, having no other possible suitor, she amused herself by playing with his heart? Why else should she resent the intrusion of another young woman, even so plain a one as I, into the house?

The Lady Dortha showed me to a small, clean room,

where I washed myself and put on the old woolen robe from my pack. I laid myself upon a bed that no king could have bettered. Sleep drowned me in its blackness, yet even in those depths I felt the pull of compulsion. Some task waited for me, before I left Orwen Deep.

I had been too overcome with weariness to wait for food. So, though I slept so well that I seemed another person entirely, I woke early to the growling in my middle. My garments had been shaken out and hung to dry, I found when I rose. I donned them and went down to join those I could hear stirring in the dawnlight.

A huge fire was roaring in the hearth, driving the night chill from the chamber. The pot hung from its hooks, and thick porridge bubbled slowly, making happy plops that sometimes fizzed moisture into the coals. Dortha was bustling about, pausing only to add dollops of butter and honey to the porridge, which Arnulf stirred occasionally as he sat on a stool and mended leather mittens.

"What may I do to help?" I asked, as I entered, bending my head to miss the lintel. "An appetite even larger than I am woke with me this morning. I must do wonders of service to earn the breakfast I crave."

"Only set the trenchers from the shelf onto the table and find the spoons in the drawer below. These winter days, Isola finds no joy in waking early, so we do not wait for her. Only the cream remains to be skimmed, and then we will eat." She took up a heavy stoneware pitcher and went into a doorway that opened, I surmised, on her dairy room, for I heard her steps clacking on stone flooring.

More than one measure of porridge, laced with honey

and stippled with thick cream, found its way into my interior, before I was done. Arnulf and Dortha all but matched me in appetite, and we set back only a small portion to keep warm for the sluggardly Isola.

Then they two turned to me, as I gathered up the soiled utensils. I could see both hope and expectation in their eyes.

"Sit, while I clean these, and I will tell you of something in my possession that might help you in your problem," I told them, pouring steaming water from a kettle into the stone trough where the dishes were washed.

As I scrubbed trenchers and spoons, I began. "Late in the fall I chanced to find myself in a wood, some weeks' journey to the south, well within the forested lands. You may or may not have heard of the witch An-Perria? Her wood it was into which I stumbled. She had some notion of trading her old and ugly carcass for my own, a matter that made me look more favorably upon my own attributes than I ever did before."

Dortha caught her breath. "Even here, the name of An-Perria has been heard. A creature of terrible malice, it is said, preying on beasts and children to supply her with the stuff of her spells. How did you escape?"

"I did not precisely escape. I boiled her in her own pot and came away with her spell-book."

"The spell-book of An-Perria?" they breathed in unison. "A great treasure, indeed."

Arnulf's pale eyes glowed beneath their curling red brows. "And do you think that you can use this book to help us? Such things can be dangerous in unskilled hands."

"I have used it only once. I believe that it worked perfectly well, that time. My intuitions tell me that I succeeded in what I attempted. But some of the receipts are so dreadful that no person in his senses would meddle with them. Still, many are fairly simple matters of using the correct herbs in conjunction with the proper ritual words. Those we might well manage, I think, if one of you is skilled in herbs. Not all that I took from An-Perria's store were marked with their names."

Dortha nodded, one brisk jerk of her gray-spangled head. "My family has always been skilled in dosing with herbs. Nothing grows on the downs or in the deep that I do not know, as well as most matters brought from far away. I can recognize most, I think."

"I have a fair sampling of her stock of dried stuff. We might go through the packets and mark the untitled with their names. Then we can look up counterspells in the book. There are those for almost any circumstance you might name. One for direwolves would be a good one to start with, if we can find it. We can always work our way forward toward a bane for Clyverrin."

"Perhaps we might find one for the protection of the sheep?" Arnulf queried. "They are in a fold at some distance and are attacked often. Yet we are too few to dispute with the direwolves when they come. They do not fear Man, as others of their kind do. They attack me or the Lady Dortha as readily as they do the sheep. We lose numbers, week by week."

While Dortha and Arnulf sorted through the herb packets, marking those in need of it, I browsed through

An-Perria's book, taking care with the ancient pages as I turned them. Many hands, over long spans of years, had added to their content. There were spells for every ill ever dreamed of by Man, both for laying them on and taking them off. There were spells for curing or making ill both people and animals, for protections and imperilments. So thick was the book and so stingy the handwriting that the volume contained what seemed to be the entire world of witchery between its stained covers.

As I had expected, I found an entire section concerning the direwolf. And not to my surprise, I learned that it was the easiest of the ferocious beasts for a wicked soul to take possession of. There were methods of bringing it hither and of sending it hence, not to mention suggestions for uses that made the hair curl on my scalp. At the bottom of the page, in tiny penmanship, there was a short footnote: For protecting a sheepfold.

I crowed aloud. My two companions looked up from their task. "Do we have in the assortment some dried peony?" I asked.

Dortha rustled through the packets and said, "We do. I wondered at it, too."

"It is powerful in the protection of shepherds and their flocks! Is there mugwort there?"

"This, I am sure, is mugwort. And there is angelica, which is a witches' bane."

"Those, set with the spell here, should protect the sheep. Then we can go on to greater things!" I cried, and the two fell to laughing at my excitement.

Although snow was falling again, Arnulf and I set

out, after a time, armed with knobstick, blade, bag and book. The sheepfold was our goal and the magic we made there was carefully done. Symbols were drawn with fingers dipped in mixtures of herbs and water. Chants that we pronounced over our efforts rang strangely in the clean air of the deep, while the sheep watched us with uncomprehending eyes. At last we were done with the business.

Looking about the fold, I could see draggled fleeces draped over the wall, where the sheep that had died beneath the fangs of the direwolves had been hastily skinned. Surveying that stout wall and its equally stout gate, I wondered aloud that any beast of the night could make its way into the place.

Arnulf grunted. "We have also wondered. We can find no answer save that the direwolves that now hunt our deep are not a natural kind. If these spells are effective, then we will know that the Clyverrin have conjured them from some fell source."

Strange as it might seem, the effort of enspelling the sheepfold had exhausted us both. We returned to Dortha's hearth with lagging steps and gladly filled ourselves with her rich soup and bread. Then we both dozed, leaning comfortably into the cushioned settles that flanked the fire, while Dortha shushed Isola's sharp voice. We slept the afternoon away, waking only when the light had grown dim.

"I must attend to the beasts," Arnulf insisted, when he had his eyes well open. "Even I hesitate to do that in darkness. Why did you not wake me?"

"Isola and I attended to that," Dortha answered. "If

the thing that you and Grittel attempted will deliver us from our perils, then you must have strength to give to it. Isola and I will do the day-work, leaving the two of you to work your enchantments and to watch their effectiveness."

That had been my waking thought: that I must watch what effect the spells might have on anything approaching the sheepfold. Turning toward Arnulf, I saw the same determination in his eyes. "In two hours it will be time to go out, if you are willing to?" he half-queried.

"If the Lady Dortha will but give me leave to attack her roast mutton and her loaf, then I will be well-sustained against anything we might find in the night," I replied.

But while I ate, I laid the spell-book beside my trencher and glanced hurriedly through it. I felt that we two would likely need some influence to cloak our presence, if we were to see truly the working of our spells. The word betony appeared often on those grimed pages, and its uses seemed many and interesting. At last I sorted through the marked packets and took out pinches of betony and rosemary, making tiny bags to hold a bit of each.

While Arnulf finished his meal, I went up to the room that held my belongings and drew from the pack the blade I had taken from Dorin Anthelles. I felt, now, that it might serve me better than my knobstick could, and, thus armed, I went down the stair to meet my companion.

VI

THE TRANSFORMATION OF THE CLYVERRIN

We set out into the cold night, into which no star peered from the clouded deeps. Long before we reached the sheepfold, we could hear indefinable stirrings and pantings about its walls. I tightened my grip on the swordhilt, my heart tapping hastily at my ribs. Almost as words, those breathy sounds came to our ears. Yet the voices were not any that could issue from human throats. Arnulf hissed softly between his teeth, and I followed him as he dropped to all fours and scuttled up a snow-clogged path that led toward the gateless side of the fold.

My blood was singing, now. The tingle of the snow as it slipped into my mittens wasn't even an annoyance. My senses seemed honed to extreme sharpness, and I could almost count the different pantings that came to me. We turned a corner, then another, to sink behind a drift, watching the activity taking place against the white backdrop of snow.

Seven shapes stained the purity of the place. They were casting back and forth, leaping toward the top of the wall, only to fall back with muffled whines. Pained frustration breathed from them, and I grinned into the night. Our amateur spell-casting was evidently holding them at bay. I could see the ease with which they made the great leaps that would have carried them over the wall, in other circumstances.

Arnulf gripped my arm tightly, pulling me deeper behind the drift. I sank with him into its concealment. It was not our purpose to confront those things, now. We simply wanted to know if the work we had done there would hold at bay the black forces of the Clyverrin. And it did.

It was well after the middle hour of night when the pack gave over its efforts and slunk away. Even then, their slobbering, panting breaths came across the snow to us with something like the effect of speech. I, at least, felt certain that those were no beasts fostered by the honest soil of the downs.

We reached the path that Garry guarded long before dawn. A word from Arnulf quieted the dog before he could give his one-note warning. We tapped at the door, and Dortha admitted us as soon as Arnulf had whispered their secret password. She had slept, fully clothed, on one of the settles, waiting for us to return. Once she knew that our first plan had succeeded, she hurried us off to our beds, but I could see that the lady was afire with purpose. If she were anything similar to me, she was thinking of her murdered husband and planning vengeance against his killers. It suited me very well to aid her in it.

It seemed that my head had hardly touched the pillow when a terrible clamor arose in the darkness. Springing up, I hurried on my boots and caught up the blade that lay beside the bed. Arnulf met me in the hallway, hair and eyes wild in the dimness. We tumbled down the stair together.

"Bar the door behind us!" he shouted to Dortha, as we hurled the heavy portal open and ran toward the byre. From that direction we could hear bellowings of agony, mixed with sharp howls.

We were traveling too fast for speech, but we both knew that those defeated beasts had in some way reported their failure. Others had been sent, hoping to take us unaware. As we ran, I thrust into Arnulf's pocket a sprig of fennel that I had caught up as I passed the small table on which the herb packets rested. If some kind of wicked spirit possessed the beasts at the byre, then that might give us some small protection.

We did not go around to enter by the gateway. Arnulf hurled himself at the wall, and over. I was just behind him. We alit in the midst of furry bodies and bawling cattle. Our blades were busy in an instant. Setting our backs together, we thrust and hacked until a pile of direwolves lay in a double arc about us.

The rest, some ten it seemed in the mottled darkness,

drew back to lick their wounds. We used the respite to huddle the kine into a corner that we could defend. Then we waited, and the gods will attest that those furred beasts conferred in almost-words as they pondered how best to attack us.

"Feel in your pocket," I breathed to Arnulf, bringing out my own fennel and gripping it between hilt and hand.

"A wolf-bane?" he asked, doing the same.

"No. One against evil spirits. If these be wolves, then they are used by spirits that are not their own. Listen to them talk, there by the gate!"

The muttering stopped abruptly. The beasts came again, this time in a wide arc. It was obvious that three, at least, would attack each of us at once, leaving the others to fill any gaps or to take advantage of any weakness in our defense. Not, I think, a wolfish sort of plan at all.

"See?" I hissed, and my companion grunted agreement.

With a flash of inspiration, I ran my sprig down my blade. Arnulf, seeing, did likewise. Then they were upon us, leaping to attack at head-height, while others dived low to take us at knee or groin.

My blade sang in the air. There was an ungodly howl, but I had no time to watch. Two were at my knee and my chest. More howls rose, and Arnulf and I stood clear. Six furred bodies twitched and slobbered at our feet. They were in some way different from the things they had seemed to be before. The four reserves slunk back, toward the gate, and we made for them, determined not to leave one alive.

With one accord, they howled and scrambled for the gate. My flung sword brought one down, as it leaped for the top of the gate. I was upon him before he could drag himself from the snow. Weirdly bright eyes glared at me as I bent toward the thing and rubbed the fennel against its nose. There was a yelp of anguish, and the eyes dimmed to animal bewilderment. Pitying, I ended its suffering and watched Arnulf bring down another. The remaining two vanished over the gate unto the dimness of dawn.

Weary past believing, we staggered, once more, toward the house and were admitted. Dortha had hot food ready, and we ate in a fog. Then we stumbled away to sleep for a while. Yet we were both up well before noon. Something about our second encounter had set me to thinking. Arnulf had also drawn some conclusions.

We sat down with the book, examining every page, no matter how gruesome, with close attention. Isola drifted about us, looking with growing disfavor at our absorption in the volume that drew our heads so close together over the pages. Though I paid close attention to the work at hand, I chuckled inwardly. Those sapphire eyes were filled with jealousy. Perhaps it had been only the lack of competition for Arnulf's regard that had made the girl so careless of him. I thought, as I scanned the crabbed hand on the pages, that if we survived our perilous plot, Arnulf might well thank me for more than mere freedom from the Clyverrin.

We had slept for such a short time, eating at irregular intervals, that our midday meal was made in the afternoon. As we sat at the table, I outlined my conclusions to Arnulf and Dortha. Isola pointedly rose and left the room when I began to speak, and I was hard put to keep from smiling. Yet serious work was at hand, and I sobered as I spoke.

"One thing becomes clearer as I study this volume. Two distinct and inimical sorts of sorcery exist. The kind that we have used, involving things of the soil combined with potent words, is a clean thing, tied in some way to the planet and the healthy things of the world. The pages holding those spells are fairly clean, which tells me that An-Perria seldom used them.

"The book is sharply divided between the sections concerning the earth-magics and those outlining the sorceries using demons, necromancy, and callings to other dimensions than our own.

"The Clyverrin are using the dark sort, do not doubt it. The direwolves we saw and slew were possessed by spirits other than their own. That is a thing the clean witchery does not allow. So we are headed aright: Using a sort of sorcery that the enemy cannot use, for they are incapable of it because of their own uncleanness, we may well be able to defeat them on their own sorcerous ground. They chose to use black forces against their neighbors. We can fight them in the misty world of magics. What do you think?"

Arnulf grunted softly, looking at Dortha. That lady nodded. "It is good sense, if such can be said of such arcane things. Our time here is short. We have known it for a long time. Without our animals, unable to till the fields in safety, we know that our days are numbered. We will be forced to flee or to surrender to the Clyverrin. It is better to die struggling against the darkness than to do either of those things."

"But will Isola agree? She is young and loves life. Will she cooperate?"

"She is no younger than you. This will be to her profit, as it will not be to yours. She is spoilt and willful, but her heart is sound. You, Grittel, involve yourself without compulsion or gain, simply to see justice done. She will do no less, when things are made clear to her."

I nodded. I had read the young woman fairly, I thought. She was less than mannerly, but her isolated life could explain that. Her problem lay in the fact that she had had no competition for Arnulf's affection. I had a sudden thought.

"It seems to me . . . correct me, if I'm wrong . . . that Arnulf looks kindly upon her. But she, miffed, it may be, at having no other choice, has not responded. I have seen her look upon me with something like jealousy, plain though I am. It might be that Arnulf, speaking now, might weld her more firmly to our efforts."

Her mother looked up, and her eyes kindled. "We have been so long faced with that problem that we did not see the solution you bring. It is obvious that she has set her bristles against you, for no reason. Surely, you are correct! She is jealous." Dortha turned her eyes toward Arnulf. "Now, if ever, is the time to offer her your heart. You have my leave and my dearest hope. Go and see if you can persuade her in the way her own heart would go, if she will allow it to."

He grunted again, very softly. Those pale eyes sparked

at me from beneath the curling brows. If I had doubted his feeling at all, my doubt would have disappeared. He rose and ran up the steps with the vigor of renewed hope. I sighed with relief.

I looked down at the volume on the table before us. "It would be well," I said, "to make a plan. And other plans, if this one should fail. I will read. You may, if you will, lay out the proper herbs for each spell as I choose it."

We spent a quiet time, though the words I read fell strangely into the warm homeliness of that room. At times the fire spurted high in thin tendrils, as some especially potent spell was spoken. Otherwise all was still. The piles of herbs grew, and I copied off the words that accompanied them, along with the purpose of each. I had no intention of becoming confused, amateur that I was, in this most dangerous of ventures.

Before nightfall, Arnulf came down the stair. His very beard beamed, and Dortha and I smiled to see him come. Isola's reply was written across his face.

When he saw what we had done, and I had explained the possible variations to our plans, he sat on the worn bench beside the table and looked at us both. "It has come to me, even in the happiness of the past hour, that we must attack the enemy in his own place. To sit waiting for their next move is no solution, even if we counter them each time. We must not wait. They know now that we have some new power that they have not found here before. They will strike at us, and hard. We must forestall them. What do you think?" His eyes turned toward me.

"How far is their hold? Can it be reached tonight?" I asked.

"If we start now, we will be there before cock-crow. My only concern is leaving my ladies unguarded, should the enemy strike tonight."

"There is a potent spell for securing a hold from temporal or spiritual attack," I answered, turning the leaves of the book. "Here! Four herbs will be needed. I will make the spell while you make ready to go. Our long legs will cover the miles speedily, I think."

I took basil, bramble, and the other things in hand, mixed them with water and wine, and went about the outside walls and windows, drawing the sacred symbols on every possible entry. The complex syllables now found their way more readily from my lips, and I noticed, astonished, that the worn brown stones brightened—seemed to harden—beneath the spell.

We left with the setting of the sun. Isola clung to Arnulf closely enough to make him blush as red as his beard and hair. But we set off through the snow, leaving the women to wait out what must be, for us all, a very long night.

We climbed from the deep onto the downs. There was still light on that high land. This allowed us to forge ahead at a good pace, and the level ways, well marked with old cart-tracks and cattle trails, aided us yet further. After full darkness fell, the sky cleared. Stars massed above, allowing us to see with fair clarity, and at a few hours after midnight we found ourselves standing against a wall that seemed to go upward forever, it was so very tall.

"We should begin here," I whispered. "If we go all around the wall, no enchantment will be able to pass it, either to go or to come. I'll go left, clockwise. You go widdershins, marking the symbols. Pause when you reach this spot again, and I will arrive soon, for I will be reading the spell."

He nodded, took the jug of mixture I had prepared, and slipped into the darkness. I turned and set my right hand against the stone. In my quietest voice, I chanted, "Ohm roghi eighha . . ." the harsh syllables rasping my throat.

It was a long way around. Dawn stood in the sky before both of us had made the circuit and met at our starting-place. I quenced my lightglass, by means of which I had read off the spell, and thrust it into my small pack. Then Arnulf sprang at the wall, caught a winter-killed vine that curled over the top, and pulled himself up. I was a bit less agile, with my great size, but I set toe in crack and fingers in cranny and joined him at the top.

We looked down on a wide straggle of overgrown lawn, thick with untrimmed shrubbery. In its midst stood a gaunt house, whose stone showed black in the dimness. No light could be seen, though smoke rose lazily from the central stack, which probably led upward from the kitchens. Fowl clacked from somewhere behind the place, and a line of dark birds sat along its guttering. Their wings were hunched, and their heads were down. I blessed the concealing herbs we had placed in our pockets, for I knew them to be watchers. No mundane dog seemed to please the Clyverrin.

We dropped softly behind the nearest tangle of bushes. I took from my pack the potion that Dortha had so carefully concocted, using chicory and ritual and words that had no meaning to either of us. A sip for Arnulf, one for me. We stood, waiting to see if our first plan could work for us. The light was growing stronger, and we, praise be to the gods, were growing dimmer. Like mists of morning, we thinned out—clothing, swords, packs, and accoutrements alike—until nothing stood where Arnulf had been. When I looked down at myself, I could see nothing there.

Locking hand to hand, so as not to lose one another, we sped toward the building. It had been a goodly house: we could see that as we neared it. The dark stain on the stone, the unkempt grounds, the paintless door and window-frames seemed to speak of long emptiness, but there was no doubt that it was tenanted. Even as we gained the rear of the place, where doors led out toward stable, fowl-run, and byre, voices could be heard within. Just ahead of us, one of the doors opened, and a sleepy boy came out, bearing a slop-pail.

Slipping past him, I caught the door before it could close. I felt my companion bump my shoulder as we both went inside. There was a stench to turn a vulture's stomach, but I held my breath and pressed on along the corridor that led from back to front, ending at wide doors that we had seen from the wall. They were securely barred. Before them sat a creature so weird that I stopped, causing Arnulf to bump into me as he, also, came to a halt. We stood for many heartbeats, calculating our chances of getting by that toadlike thing that stretched before it a man's legs and arms. Its body, unlike head or limbs, had something of the shape of a hound. It was, all in all, a formidable thing to meet on an errand such as ours.

While I stood wondering, Arnulf's bulk was gone from beside my elbow. The creature's eyes peered about, as if it had been startled from its doze. And then its head leaped from the dog-shoulders and landed on the floor in a splatter of dark blood. A seasoned warrior is a convenient companion, I decided, as I followed the quiet sound of his feet on the stair.

There were doors on both sides of the corridor above. It was impossible to know if the rooms were occupied, so we marked each of them with a symbol. Then I stood at the end of the corridor and spoke the great spell that I had chosen.

"Caerh Ihm Reahi! Caerh ahih shsha. Uhi lohirril; uhi narrohla; uhi ihm caerh garrahi!"

There was a moment of almost-tangible silence. Then a loud squawking arose from above the windows that opened onto the front of the house. The watchers swooped awkwardly across the glazed openings, their membranous wings flapping dismally. With raucous cries, they fled through the new sunlight toward the distant wall—and dropped out of the air just short of it.

"An-Perria is boiling still, if she knows that her spell book is working for good," I said.

The doors along the hall now began to open. The first was thrust wide by a long arm. A tall man in a bedgown strode forth. Yet as he passed the marked door panel, he began to shrink. By the time he stood fully in the hallway, he was an almost dwarfish figure, gnarled and ugly. Looking down at himself, he began to shriek vile oaths, mixed with what I knew must be some kind of spell.

There was no result. He leaned against the wall, his chin against his chest, as another pushed past him, blade in hand. This scarred warrior looked about wildly, as he shouted, "To me! We are attacked with witchery! To me, all of Clyverrin!"

Then his blade engaged with a zing, and he was fighting for his life with an invisible enemy. Behind him came another, and I sprang past to hold him from Arnulf's unseen back. Four more joined the melee, and with our invisibility, as often as not, we could maneuver them into engaging one another. As they staggered about in the half-light of the corridor, I saw the chance to seize the dwarf who had come forth first. I caught him up in my arms and sprang for the stair.

"Come, Arnulf!" I cried. "This is the one we need!"

By the time he joined me outside the door wherein we had entered, he was beginning to show as a shadow in the sunlight. I handed the dwarf to him and turned toward the house. I fumbled another packet of herbs from my pouch and hurled it into the doorway, shouting, "Krikkitikilli! Kallikitalli; Illakatilli!" And the hall burst into flames.

I caught up my prisoner more firmly, though he was struggling mightily, while Arnulf found his breath and peered around the corner of the now-blazing house. He grunted commandingly, and I took to my heels in his wake. A boil of angry Clyverrin swarmed after us from the now-opened front door. They were large men, tough-looking and battle-scarred. But we outran them to the wall.

There, however, we knew that we must stop and stand them down. Getting over that wall was no easy feat, particularly with a prisoner. I set the dwarfed Clyverrin down and bound his hands and feet with things from my pack. Then we turned our backs upon him and his stony bastion, facing those who came.

Now that we could be seen (though there were still thin spots in Arnulf's outline, and most likely in my own), those pursuers were less avid for an encounter. They fanned out and came cautiously. Their tactics were so similar to those of the wolves of the previous night that I wondered whose spirits, indeed, had tenanted those hapless beasts' bodies. But I had little time to think on it, for they came, as before, two at each of us and the fifth standing by, watching for an opportunity to take one of us unaware.

They were skilled bladesmen. Only my long reach and my tireless muscles allowed me to hold my own with them, since I had not been trained in swordplay as a profession, as they had evidently been. A lucky thrust rid me of the bolder of the two, and the fifth man filled his place. Sweat and the clash of blades filled the world for a time. I felt my back muscles beginning to tire, and my legs moved less nimbly. Then I cut the feet from under the taller man and turned to attend to the other. From the corner of my eye, I saw that one of Arnulf's foes was crawling rapidly toward the house, from which a thin haze of smoke was beginning to seep.

At that moment, there came a shrilling of women's voices. Both our opponents backed off, listening. As one, they turned and ran for the house, where fire now showed at the windows on the lower floor. Even the wounded were striving to reach the structure.

I looked after them and said, "We really should follow and finish them off, men and women alike."

Arnulf nodded, his disordered red curls flying in the breeze. "You speak truly. Yet such is not my way . . . nor yours, I think. They are in distress, and we would lessen our worthiness to work the clean magics, if we pursued them now."

I grinned at him, feeling a kinship that I had seldom felt in my short life. Lifting our captive, I nodded toward the wall.

"I'll go first," the red-beard volunteered. "You can toss him over the wall to me, when I shout."

In less time than one would have thought, we were all three on the right side of the stone barrier. Our prisoner shrank even more and grew even more gnarled and ugly, as he was passed over that enspelled structure. So hideous was he that my heart was moved to pity. What wonder was it that one thus slighted by nature should turn upon a world into which he could never be welcomed? And yet . . . and yet he was the source, I was certain, of the terrible suffering and injustice that had overtaken all the former inhabitants of the downs.

"Have you the book?" asked Arnulf. I could tell, from his expression, that he had something of my own feeling.

Silently, I offered him the volume from my pack. The breeze fluttered the pages, as Arnulf turned through, seeking some specific spell. I could remember none that might solve this specific problem, but I said nothing.

Then came his voice, reading from the book: "A cleansing of diseased spirit. This, if anything, can cure yon manikin of his evil. Find the packet that you made up of the healing and cleansing herbs."

We bound the little man to a tree almost as dwarfed as himself, in the bitter winds of the downs. I took from the packet many herbs: betony, plantain, Solomon's seal, and more. As Arnulf read from the book, I arranged them in patterns upon the dried ferns we had piled in a circle, well away from the tiny feet.

Arnulf handed the book to me. I read the words, sounding them carefully, as he knelt to light the heal-fire.

"Aralillia emphurat saralla . . . empheor enhallia . . . maret alla . . ." It was a long spell, intricate and strangely beautiful. I felt that with only a slight nudge, my mind could comprehend its meaning. The cold wind that now blew took on a cleanliness that it had not had before, as the words and the smokes mingled and enwreathed the writhing dwarf.

The herbs blazed high, making more fire than the amount of fuel seemed to warrant. We two stood amazed at the change that now overtook our captive. The twisted deformity began to smooth away, very gradually. As the smoke that wrapped him about was carried toward his wall, its character, too, changed. The stone aged and crumbled before our eyes. A long crack opened, allowing clumps of stone to fall inward.

Looking through that opening, we could see that the house was now an oven, though to our relief the men were busy on the lawn, carrying women and infants from the reach of the flames. Seeing this, our captive cried out. A last burst of fury sparked in his eyes. Then he fainted and sagged against his bonds.

We loosed him and laid him on the snow. To our wonder, he now seemed totally different, both from the tall and the dwarfed selves we had seen. He was merely a tiny man, worn and ill, who lay there. The taint of evil that had breathed from his being was gone with the smokes that had banished it.

"They are only people, now," Arnulf said.

I nodded agreement. "Perhaps cruel people, people who may yet covet what their neighbors have, but, I think, ones who cannot again call up black forces to aid in their endeavors. This was the Clyverrin, here at our feet. With his cleansing, there will be none who can work the dark magics." I looked down at him, feeling again a dim pity.

Arnulf bent to lift the still figure in his arms. "I'll put him inside the wall," he said. "His followers will find him, or he will go to them when he wakes. It may be that they will turn on him, now that his black powers are gone. He may become their slave, or their victim. Still, he collected them from all the lands about. His is the responsibility for their being here in one place. His is the penance. Be certain that we will watch this place closely, summer and winter, to see that none again goes in forbidden ways."

We turned back across the downs, slowly, this time, with our bones protesting their punishment. As a new snow began to fall into the young darkness, we approached the house. Garry spoke his warning, only to be shushed by Arnulf. The door opened in the darkness, and welcome light and warmth spilled out to greet us.

We sighed and shook our heads, pushing away into the recesses of memory the recollection of our work of the day. We were home again, and that was enough.

VII

THE THING UPON THE MOORLAND

It was good to set my foot on the uplands again. The winter had been a good one, secure enough, once the threat of the Clyverrin was removed from the farmstead. The Lady Dortha and I had studied the spellbook and the herbs I had taken from An-Perria's store until we felt that we knew almost as much of the lore as she—perhaps more, since she had evidently been uninterested in the more healthful applications. The dark side of the art we investigated, with particular attention to methods of circumventing it.

I had left amid regrets from the Lady Dortha and relief from Isola. Not that she admitted as much, but even though the marriage-words had been pronounced by her mother and Arnulf, even though Arnulf was as devoted a husband as any could wish, still she viewed me as a potential rival. I didn't know whether to be complimented or amused. Surely that, more than anything, proved how isolated her life had been. She had no standard against which to measure me.

Arnulf had walked a few leagues with me, checking the outer fringes of the hold for strayed cattle or sign of direwolves. But those beasts had disappeared with the un-fanging of the Clyverrin. There was no sign in all the way of any except the small, timid creatures that roamed the uplands and the fells.

We parted on a ridge overlooking the entire sweep of moor and fell. This was at the edge of the high moors, and beyond this place the land was wild, untenanted, as far as he knew. He had tried for weeks to dissuade me from going in that direction.

"There will be no farms, no keeps, no people except, possibly, some wild, mad hermits or outlaws who have been driven from more orderly ways. Stay with us, or turn toward the sea. I will worry, when you are gone. As will our lady mother."

I smiled at him. He was the first man in my acquaintance, save my father, who had looked at me with the eyes of a friend and comrade. Whose gaze had not roved down my shape instead of reading my character in my plain face. I had much affection for the big red-beard. If matters had been arranged differently . . . I had a wistful vision of a row of red-headed cherubs, but I instantly blanked it away. That door was closed to me by nature. Still, I hugged him, lifting him from his feet in my exuberance.

"I will send word, if there is opportunity," I told him. "But I am wandering the world, and this is the direction that calls to me. No one knows what is there, for none have traveled that way for many lives of men. Now I will see for myself what mysteries move upon the moorlands and the mountains beyond. Do not fear for me. What safer companions could there be than my knobstick, my blade, and my spell-book?"

He had returned my hug, slapped my big shoulder. I knew that he watched me out of sight, though I did not turn to see. I knew quite well that my own eyes were damp. Seeing him there would have undone me, I was sure.

The moors opened out widely for leagues. Except for an occasional hill and some standing rocks of trollish shape, the expanse before me was empty. The low bushes and stubby vegetation blended into the gray-green distances, struck into mottled streaks by the spring sun. The air was intoxicating, clean and vigorous and untainted by the smokes of man-fires. I stepped out gladly, my big feet in their well-made boots (fresh from the cobbling of Arnulf) crushing spring blossoms into the surrounding grass.

Night found me camped beneath a purple-black stub of stone that reared its ugly shape toward the chilly stars. Spring was not long advanced, and I built a fire of brush and weeds, as much for the warmth as for heating rations of dried meat. But when it began to die, I did not replenish it. I rolled myself in the fleece cloak I had been given by the Lady Dortha and leaned against the stone, watching the stars roll away over the horizon. Never had I been in a land whose sky had been so wide, so open, so free. It spoke to me compellingly, beckoning me onward into its mysteries.

My eyes were growing heavy, and I was about to pillow my head on my pack when a bright blaze of light soared across the arc of sky at which I had been staring. The Fisherman's net held, for an instant, a brighter catch than his usual dim swarm of stars. I sat up, following the spark until it was quenched at the edge of the world.

"There?" I asked myself.

"There!" my innermost instincts replied. I felt that I had been given a sign by some power even greater than those that answered to the arts of An-Perria.

I huddled the fleece about my ears and closed my eyes. Tomorrow I would go northwestward, in line with a distant tor. Perhaps I might find the shattered remains of the star-stone that had fallen. Probably not, but at least it gave some direction to my wandering path.

As soon as my eyes opened to the new morning, I remembered my vision. Looking away to the northwest, I could see the tor by which I had sighted. It seemed even bigger than it had when it was bulked, black, against the thickly starred sky. Unwilling to waste any time, I nibbled dried fruit, drank from my bottle of water mixed with herbs, and put my pack together. With the sun on my shoulders, I went toward the dark blot on the horizon behind which the streak of light had fallen.

Something more than curiosity drove me. Since beginning to dig into the spell-book and its attendant rituals and mysteries, I had found myself growing intuitive. Topping a roll of land, I would have a dim prevision of what lay beyond. Even the thoughts of others had begun to open themselves to me, though I had not mentioned that to any at Orwen Deep. Such talents, while not unkown among our folk, are considered uncomfortable in those nearest to you.

Now, as I went among the ankle-deep grasses of spring, I felt multiple tiny impulses about me. Small minds of unseen creatures were busy beneath rocks and among the gorse and the big tough whip-grasses. To my delight, I caught a fleeting glimpse of this high world from the elevated eye of a carrion-eater that was soaring out of sight to my own eyes. And in that instant's span, I saw something that was still beyond my horizon. Something strange, shining, metallic. Beyond the tor.

Dizzied by the unusual experience, I paused to blink my vision straight. Something had fallen, true. I had thought it to be only another of the many stones that fall from the sky; according to the tutor of my youth, they were fragments of other worlds in our thickly tenanted spaces. The Visionaries intuited this, both from observed evidence and from their unique gifts.

But what lay upon the flattish plain beyond that towering stone pillar was no thing of stone. The moorlands, I dared to think, had never seen anything quite like it. Had the Visionaries? I had not been taught so, if they had.

I hurried onward and did not stop at midday to rest or to eat. By late evening, I was drawing near to the rock that was my guide. It bulked hugely above my way. Like those others I had passed, it was purple-black, scarred by time, weather, and strange scorings that might have been markings made by men. Yet no men had lived upon the moors in all our history, or even in the folk myths that hold the more ancient past. I had a feeling about those markings, but it was too ill-defined to make sense of. So I ignored my intuitions and set my long legs to covering space at an amazing clip.

By the time it was too dark to travel safely, I had reached the foot of the stone. I made camp against it, on the side away from the plain beyond. A small fire was kindled in a curving outcrop, and in its heat I gratefully warmed water in my small pot and made a stew of dried meat and fruit. Such efforts as I had made that day depleted the flesh, and I knew that I might well need exceptional energies in the day ahead.

When I woke, a layer of high cloud had dimmed the spring morning. There was a nip from the north, brought down from the unseen mountains by a wind sharper than my blade. I was glad of my fleeces as I angled into that chilly draft, making for the point at which I believed I might find that bright shape I had seen from above.

Once well past the towering stone, I could see far out across the flattened saucer that was the plain. And it seemed that I could detect, at the very edge of vision, a glimmer, dulled by the cloudy light, but no part of the natural lights and shadows of the land ahead. A metallic sheen. I had not a doubt of it.

The day wore past, as the last had done, in swinging strides that I divorced from thought. Twice I dug meat from my pack to bolster me in my efforts, but I didn't stop. Something was whispering to me that there was a need for me, there beside that distant thing that sat upon the moor.

Night came down more swiftly than the last had done.

A patter of rain made me lift the hood over my head and fasten down the flaps of my pack, to keep out the wet. There were no stars to guide me, as darkness grew thicker, but I didn't need them now. For there was a glow from the shape that was now well within range of my sight.

And even above the slight whisper of the rain, there was other sound. Voices, low-pitched but clear, speaking unfamiliar syllables. Clinks of metal against metal. A sputtering sound, not unlike meat frying in a pan. There were people there, no doubt of that. I hesitated. Who might they be, to come riding down the sky in a craft of metal? We were carefully taught from childhood to be sparing of that precious stuff, to use blade and knife, pot and lance-head until it was worn past use, then to make it into something else to use again. Our world, we well knew, was poor in such material.

Whoever they were, it might be unwise to come upon them out of the dark and unannounced. I had had more than one member of my own race meet me with suspicion and hostility, on account of my size. These people might well have the same attitude.

There was no comfortable spot in which to take shelter. Grateful for my impervious fleeces, I went to earth beneath a tangle of whip-grass, wrapping it together above my head to keep out the worst of the persistent drizzle. Evidently those I was approaching had no intention of sleeping, or they did it in shifts and by turns. There was no lessening of the quiet busyness from the spot where the blue-white brightness glowed.

With first light I was up, wringing damp from the

edges of my cloak and my hood, making the best toilette I could after sleeping amid the grasses. Across the distance now left, I could see occasional movement on the very strange creation that stood, ungainly yet oddly graceful, on the plain.

I went forward boldly, hands out from my sides and conspicuously empty. I had gone less than a dozen paces when a voice roared at me. I took the words to mean HALT, and I did so at once. I could see clearly, now, the beings I confronted. The one who had called out was pointing at me a slender tube that I took to be a weapon. Another had joined it, appearing from an opening that had loomed where only shiny metal had been before. Four more of them came down a sort of stair or ladder from that round hole and stood staring at me.

I held my hands far from my sides and went forward, quite slowly. I cannot now explain why I felt so compelled to face these creatures, to examine their craft, but I was in the grip of a compulsive intuition. The skills that I had learned from An-Perria's book had opened me to forces that I did not yet understand. I recognized that, even as I went forward.

I felt their minds! How strange it seemed to touch thought-processes so like my own, yet so unlike. Words were there, though they meant nothing to me as yet. But there were also pictures, emotions, a turmoil of feeling. I was staggered and overwhelmed, for a moment, by the multiple images I faced. I stopped and put my hands to my eyes, trying to stop the overlapping impressions.

The voice spoke again, more softly. I brought my

hands level with my shoulders, unstrapped my pack and let it fall. The drizzle had stopped, and a light breeze was rippling my heavy cloak. I untied its thongs and let it, too, fall to the grass.

"By God, she's a woman! Biggest one I ever saw!" The words were foreign, but I was able to read their meaning all too clearly. For a moment the old anger rose in me. Then I quelled it. Why should these be different from my own people? I gestured toward the craft, raised my hand in a questioning motion, then described an arc with my arm, following the track that had brought them to this spot. I pointed away toward the tor, which was, once again, small in the distance. By signs, I indicated that I had seen their coming to earth and had come to investigate.

A hand was raised, in their turn, by the first to challenge me. He raised one finger and pointed it at me. Then another, gesturing toward the spot from which I had come. And another.

I waggled my hands to show that there were no others. The six of them gathered into a huddle. I could see, now, that two of them were women, though all wore the same close-fitting clothing that seemed to flow evenly over body, arms, and legs, with no visible openings. I wondered how they managed to take them off. Or if they took them off at all? Unsanitary, if true.

While they huddled, I looked off across the plain, past the metal craft. And there, at about the distance of the tor I had passed, rose another. It gave me the same shiver of almost-recognition as had the first. There was something, some emanation from the things, that touched a new-found sense in me.

I turned my attention back to the conferring strangers. The wariness and confusion that I had read in them was subsiding to a tentative acceptance. I let my hands drift quietly down. Then I sat on the damp grass and watched as they made signs with their hands and babbled in their odd language. One detached himself from the group and climbed the stair into the opening. He returned, very quickly, with a contrivance of rods and glass and metal.

One of the women now turned and walked cautiously toward me. I rose to meet her and gave her greeting. She looked up at me, her eyes calculating the difference in our respective elevations. She came to a point between the second and third thongs on my tunic.

She motioned toward the group that now stood as if waiting for us. I nodded and went to stand before them. They had brought a small table from someplace not immediately evident, along with a chair that looked entirely too skeletal to hold my considerable weight. I looked at it, at them, and down at myself. The woman nodded.

Well, it was their chair. If it broke under me, it would be damaged more than I. I sat carefully and found, to my astonishment, that it was made entirely of metal, coated with a green substance. What metal-rich world would make furniture of the precious stuff?

They handed me a crownlike arrangement of glass and wire, and the woman showed me how to fix it to my head, though my thick braids were a bit of a problem. Once

I had it properly set, I found that I understood the words in their thoughts. Amazing!

I formed words awkwardly, but I spoke before any of them had time to. "How wonderful! A machine that makes different tongues understandable. Does it do this for minds more . . . unlike . . . than ours?"

They stood as if stunned. The first, whom I now perceived to be a leader among them, stepped forward and looked first at the equipment, then at me. "How did you *do* that? We're supposed to talk for a long time, then you, then the two make connections. How did you pick up our words?"

"Why, from your thoughts. Do you not have those who are skilled so?"

"Some . . . claim to be," he said. "Well, this is a different world in a different scheme of things entirely. Maybe things we thought to be impossible back where we came from can happen here."

"What . . . is . . . dimension? I cannot quite grasp what you mean by that, as you are thinking it." I frowned up at him, trying hard to understand his meaning.

He turned a little pale, which made his skin very pale, indeed, in contrast with my tanned-gold coloring. "That's a concept—I think we'd better get to know each other better and learn how to communicate more easily before we take that up. It's complicated. But before we go any further, are there people like you in this area of your world?"

I read his unease. "The moorlands are untenanted in all our history," I reassured him. "I am here because I am a wanderer. You were shocked by my size. I read it in you.

Be assured that I am larger than any of my own kind that I have ever seen. I am a . . ." I searched his mind for the right term. ". . . freak. Yes. That is what I am in this kingdom. It is what I would be in any of those upon the other two continents. Garetha holds no other that I know of like me." My tone must have been bitter, for one of the women, a taller, very dark woman, touched my shoulder as if to comfort me.

"We have some who are called that in our own worlds," the man said. "I am Carl. What may we call you?"

Then I realized how uncourteous I had been. I stood, careful not to disarrange the crown, and bowed my head carefully. "Grittellia Floresca, daughter of the Lord of Sundoth, far to the south. Renegade daughter, giantess, would-be sorcerer, and, I sometimes think, fool." I laughed.

Something in the atmosphere relaxed. The tension, the wariness went out of them.

"Come into the ship, Grittelia. You are damp and chilly. We have warmth and food there."

"I call myself Grittel," I said. "And I would dearly like to see inside this great craft of yours." I reached up and detached the crown from my head.

"Now I can read you clearly, and there is no more need of this marvelous machine. It only needs that I find more words in your tongue. Your thought is so clear to me that I can match it, in many cases, with the correct sounds." They were staring at me as if I were a freak in more than size, but there was no feel of peril about them. Now that I felt more deeply into them, in fact, I recognized something like terror and despair.

As we climbed the steep ladder, I asked Carl, "Are you troubled? I read dismay in all of you."

He reached a hand to help me into the strange, rounded room above the opening. "We are that. And we can't find our trouble, which makes it worse. The ship should be operational. It just—doesn't do anything. The power is ample. The circuits are clear. But the thing won't move."

Much of what he had said was obscure to me, though I realized that the technical details of the craft would be quite beyond my understanding. But something prodded me. The intuition again.

"Do you understand what brought you to this place? What force, what flaw in your machines might have done this?"

"Everything was optimal," he said. "We were set to warp back into normal space, and then something seemed to grab us. Sucked us through, out of the normal warp procedure, out of anything we have star-maps for, into something that Wolfert is certain is another dimension entirely."

I didn't understand much of what he said, except for the sudden pulling away from normality into an alien place. I had much of the same feeling, myself. And I began to see, not clearly but with increasing conviction, the source of that.

I turned to the tallest man in the group, who was the Wolfert he had spoken of. "Did you see, far off when I pointed, the tall stone?" He nodded. "And do you know that another is visible in the opposite direction?"

He nodded again. His eyes brightened. A furrow grew

between his light brows. "You think those might be the cause?"

"It is possible. They are marked—or the one I camped beneath was marked. With markings that mean something, though I have not the knowledge to read them. But they are strong, make no mistake. Even my new perceptions felt them clearly."

Carl was staring at me. "What are you getting at?"

I looked at him, bewildered.

"Exactly what do you mean? Is there some field those things generate? Some power?"

Ah! Now I understood. "Power, yes. It reeks of sorcery. You have been caught, I am beginning to think, in a vast web. Set, perhaps, so long ago that its setter is gone from this world. Or perhaps not."

"Sorcery!" He snorted. "Grittel, I don't know what superstitions you have on this world, but we learned long ago that sorcery is just fakery mixed with skills that misguide the onlooker."

I sorted through his mind, this time on a deeper level than I had done before. Then I sat on another of the metal chairs and grunted. "It is not strange that you would think that. I have looked into what you know of your own world's sorceries, and they seem very inept and heavy-handed. But here, on Garetha, sorcery is a real thing. I have spoken, myself, with a child who had been stolen away from another dimension. And I sent her back by the use of the same sort of witchery that brought her here. I own the spell-book of An-Perria, who was one old and learned in the arts. It may be that the thing that works in your own place does not work here. And that what does not truly exist there, does truly exist here. Is that not possible?"

He looked about at the others, who had seated themselves upon a circle of the chairs about us. I could see the doubt in their faces and in his. But I knew that I was correct. No Visionary could have seen it more clearly.

VIII

piNNACLES
of poweR

The interior of the curious craft in which these people had come to Garetha was rich with metals. To one reared on our metal-poor planet, it seemed an incredible lavishness, until Carl explained to me that their worlds, across the strange gap that separated our dimensions, were laden with metals of all sorts. And even those worlds that they could not inhabit were mined for their minerals. It seemed more magical to me than our everyday magics of Garetha until I realized that on their worlds they had neither belief in such things nor those who, like our Visionaries, saw beyond the scope of their senses.

More and more I came to know that I had been correct in my first assessment. The dividing-line between their place and mine was also a sort of terminus. We had no interest in traveling to the planets that shone in our heavens. We knew what they were, we understood their places in the balance of things, but we had no curiosity about them beyond that. And if we had possessed such curiosity, we had not the materials with which to build ships like Carl's. Or the kind of mental bent that could design them.

On the other hand, they were without the sorts of things that we had been given instead of minds and metals to go exploring worlds. It took a great deal of talk before they would even grant so much as a supposition that I knew whereof I spoke.

The clinching factor, I think, was the question that I asked Wolfert. "You have told me that your investigations show you no reason why this craft should not rise and go about its business. Nothing is wrong. True?"

He looked closely at me, his brows drawn together. But he said, "True."

"Then if nothing within your scope has disabled it, it seems that something *outside* the things you know must have done so. Is that not logical?"

His face was thunderous. I knew his sort from among my own acquaintance. That kind does not take kindly to the upsetting of their dearly held convictions. He did not want to admit that my question was valid; but he was honest, for all his prejudice, and he finally nodded.

"If you will allow, I feel it will save much time and trouble if I show you the kind of magic that is done here. It is not, believe me, a commonplace thing. Any more than I suspect your own professions are commonplace among your kind. Not incredibly rare, not at all. Just not achieved by everyone upon the road or in each hall. It is a skill that must be studied and practiced. I am not much more than a beginner at it, but I have found that I possess much aptitude for it. Having been cheated in comeliness and over-endowed with size, I find it only fair that I be given some sort of usable compensation." I looked about at the group.

The smaller woman, Leah, raised one eyebrow and nodded slowly. "I think we should let her demonstrate, Carl. We are not in our own place. That is beyond question. And it isn't unheard-of for things to be found in far-off places that have never been credited among the Amalgamated Fellowship of the Galaxy."

I smiled. Her mind, I had found, was not unlike my own in many ways. She was the easiest of all for me to read, and I had begun to suspect that she read me, to some extent, without realizing it.

To my relief, Carl and Wolfert, after conferring with Anna, the other woman, agreed to a demonstration—outside the ship, which suited me well. Who knew what reaction two magics confined into the same space might bring about?

I agreed hastily, and we clambered down the ladder-stair, to find my pack still lying where I had left it. The spell-book (wrapped, now, in oiled linen to preserve the ancient leather of its covers) came forth into my hand as if glad to be there. I looked about at my companions, wondering what spell might impress them sufficiently to force them to look at my dimension as it was.

Fire? They had fantastic ways of making that, as I had seen in my brief tenancy of their ship. There were no evil spirits (I devoutly hoped) about us to force into flight. And if there had been, I doubted that they would have recognized them as what they were. I turned through the soiled pages, past the necromantic section, into the herbal rituals. A title caught my eye: For clearing the head.

Carl had a bad case of sniffles. Once inside the craft, he had swallowed a small pill for the purpose, he told me, of keeping his nose clear. I looked at him closely, and the tip of his nose was once again beginning to turn pink. He sniffed unconsciously.

"Would you like for me to clear your head?' I asked him. "There is a spell here for that."

"I won't swallow any unholy messes!" he said.

"No, that isn't the way these things work. You just stand there—no, I see it says to sit cross-legged—and let me sprinkle the herbs in a circle around you, while saying the spell. Very simple."

Looking very doubtful, he lowered himself onto the frosted turf and sat, while I walked around him, sprinkling betony, pyramus, and chicory, crumbling it between my fingers.

The spell was an odd one, almost humorous in its effect upon me. "Leeheeya firu. Ahlaya incremi nitis ferrant. Eehleeya enfiru." An odd light-headedness almost made me stagger, and I turned to look at Carl.

And stopped in mid-stride, appalled.

I could see through his skull. More and more clearly. The rest of him was there, solid and secure. Only his head was slowly evaporating into the clear air of the moor.

None of the others seemed able to speak, so I said, quite calmly, "How do you feel, Carl?"

His shoulders turned, along with the last faint ghost

of his skull. "You know, something feels different. No post-nasal drip. Head *feels* clear. Probably psychosomatic."

I could feel his gaze on me, but no eyes were visible, now. I glanced up at Leah. Her eyes met mine, and to my astonishment there was a hint of laughter in them.

"Let me get a mirror, Carl," she said, "so you can see what is going on."

She fled up the steps, and I could have sworn I heard a giggle from the top of the ladder.

We waited in strained silence for her to return. Carl rose, stretched his legs, and shrugged exaggeratedly. His hands went to his head, and I held my breath, but there evidently was something there to his touch, for he seemed unaware of the thing that had happened to him.

Leah, rather pink about the cheeks, came back with a small glass and held it up before her commander. "Take a look, Carl. I think you'll be convinced, at long last, that witchcraft works. And works unexpectedly, too!" She was shaking slightly with suppressed laughter.

The shoulders squared before the mirror. The hands reached out to take it from hers. It tilted this way and that, angled up and down. There was a long, long silence.

"What . . . has . . . happened . . . to . . . my . . . head?" he asked, at last.

I swallowed painfully. "Spells can be tricky things," I said, a bit weakly. "You really need to know all the ins and outs of their titles. It *said* to clear the head. I took that to mean the normal kind of thing. Evidently witches don't quite mean that. Though from what you say it did do the task I intended. It just did . . . more."

"Oh, it cleared my head all right," he barked. "In every possible sense. I can breathe freely. I am thinking more clearly than ever before in my life. And I can see right through skull and brain and skin and hair as if they weren't there at all. It cleared my head and *then* some!" His stance was tight, his hands clenched on the handle of the mirror.

"Now do something about it!"

But something else occurred to me. "Could this have happened, by any known means, in your system?" I asked him.

His answer was not among the terms that I had assimilated from their minds, so far. In point of fact, it went on at some length, and I began to realize that he was doing a rather nice job of cursing me, the planet, and quite likely our entire dimension quite thoroughly. I waited, knowing from long experience that men find this therapeutic in times of stress.

The others had huddled together. Their expressions, alien as they were, could not be read easily. Yet I felt no hostility from them. Rather, they, too, seemed to be restraining laughter. Could it be that they were enjoying the discomfiture of their superior? He had struck me as a decent sort, but it was probable that a long term of confinement in limited space might make anyone seem arbitrary and unreasonable.

When he was silent, I said, "I can only look into the book. And hope that I will be able to find a title that may be what we want. As it concerns your head, we must be much more careful than we have been. And I am truly sorry for causing you such inconvenience."

"Inconvenience!" he shrieked. "I lose my head, and you call it an inconvenience? Look through your triple-damned book and find something to bring me back to normal!"

I tried very hard to do just that. Plumping myself down onto the dampish grass, I thumbed through the spell-book, which now seemed thrice as thick as ever before. Spells swam before my eyes. For curing dropsy, for inducing flatulence, for destroying crops, for any and every usage, good or evil, except the one I most needed. There was nothing at all about restoring a head to visibility. One or two seemed to hint at something useful, but I was so shaken by my terrible error that I didn't dare to try anything that was not a surety.

At last I looked up from the book and sighed. The vacant space above Carl's collar glared back at me. I could tell that he knew, just from the set of his shoulders.

"I cannot do this alone. As I told you, I am only a beginner at this. We must find an adept. Better yet, a Visionary. Someone, indeed, who is skilled and knowledge-able at this. I dare not take the chance of sending you, lone and bare, into some alien dimension, or of doing some greater harm to you in this one. I was foolish to try this way of proving the truth to you. The easily recognized spells that I have used in the past were enough to give me false confidence. I hope that you will forgive me."

There was a stifled snort from Carl. The others, their

faces sober now, moved about us, as if to give us the support of their presence, if nothing else.

When he spoke, his voice was quite calm. I remembered what he had said about thinking more clearly than ever before and was heartened as I listened.

"You believe that you can find someone who is expert at this kind of thing?" he asked. "There actually are people here who specialize in this . . . field?"

"Naturally. I presume that there are those in your own spaces who specialize in the forces that make your craft move through the ways it traverses?" He nodded. "Just so do we have those who study the forces that provide the power of our world. And, if those two pinnacles within sight of this spot mean anything, in these days, there is another one not too far away. Of course, they may be remnants of some trap set by one long departed from all our dimensions. Yet spells . . . spells tend to dissipate, over the years. I hardly believe that one could remain strong enough to pull you through from your own place unless it was continually renewed."

Leah and Wolfert nodded very solemnly, as if the thought made sense to them. Anna wrinkled her brow and looked skeptical. Carl looked blank, which was understandable.

"Have you any idea where to look for this—this adept?" he asked me.

I looked out across the moor to the peak that I had passed, then in the opposite direction toward that other. "If there is a third of those pinnacles, then I may be able to find a direction quickly. Is it possible to get up on top of your craft? To give a good view of the country to the north of us?"

Wolfert reached down a hand and hauled me to my feet. "Come with me," he said with a grunt.

We went around to the other side of the metal ship, and there, angling crazily up the side, was a skeletal ladder. "Access frame," he said. "Lets us go out to check vital points when we're in space, if there's a need. Can you climb it?"

I looked up at the lowest point of the spindly thing. Would it hold me? was the question in my mind. But I knew that, being metal, it would hold far more than a wooden one of such dimensions might do. I sprang as high as I could and caught the rod, pulling myself up to sit, then to stand on it. Without looking back at Wolfert, I went up the thing swiftly, setting my feet awkwardly on rods and braces obviously meant to be walked or clung-to from different angles than this one.

But it led to the nose of the thing. Bracing my back against the curvature, I looked northward, feeling that there must be one of the purple-black pylons there, if only I were high enough to see it.

I almost missed it. It was at such a distance that only the tip of its sharp top cleared the horizon. But it was there, quite definitely, and in the quarter where my instinct told me it must be positioned.

Satisfied, I clambered down the side of the ship and jumped the last few yards to rejoin Wolfert. "It's there,"

I told him. "Now I must look up the triangulating spell. And we'd better hurry—the sun is beginning to get low. I'm not expert enough to do this at night."

We hurried back around to the spot where we had left the others, only to find that they had been sent about their duties by Carl. He waited alone for our return. With what I considered to be great restraint, he did not ask me what I had found, as I pulled Dorin's blade from my pack, tucked it under my arm, and flipped carefully through the spell-book again.

Once I had found the proper part, I turned and spoke to him. "I hope to find what we need by use of triangulation. This is a complicated spell, using the power of those pylons, focused through metal and then radiated outward to seek their power-source. Only when three points of energy are within range can it be done. And by this fact alone I am certain that a spell brought you here, for you are all but in the exact center of the triangle formed by the peaks. The land rises a bit to north, which is what made the third hard to locate."

By the motions of his shoulders, I saw that he nodded. "We use something similar in planetary navigation, and even in space for locating distress signals. I am . . . interested . . . if you don't mind my watching."

"As you are the one most concerned, I think it only fair that you watch. Just be very still, for I must concentrate. An adept could do this and carry on a conversation, but I am not so skilled. Come—see that little hummock? That is far enough from the craft to avoid any interference from its metal, yet near enough to the center of the triangle to be effective." I turned back toward the point and hurried toward it.

Carl and Wolfert followed, but I heard the commander give a sharp order, and the taller man turned back toward the ship. Then only Carl followed me out onto the moor.

IX

A spell for finding

The small rise was well within view of two of the pylons and would have been in sight of the third, without the aforementioned gentle rise in the contour of the moor. I took my place upon it and motioned for Carl to keep some tens of paces distant.

Rereading the spell three times to fix it in my memory, I wrapped the book again and set it at my feet. The blade in my hand felt chilly and forbidding, as I brought it up to eye-level and balanced it across my palm. Then I turned very slowly to face each of the peaks in turn, and the blade moved on my hand as I turned.

I opened my mouth to begin . . . and stopped for a moment, filled with fear. This was no gentle spell of natural herbs and strange words. This was a thing of the fires and forces of nature, borrowing the stuff of lightnings and wild winds. I had never before tried to use such strong things, and my courage wavered for a moment. Then I looked down at Carl's hopeful stance and absent face. What I had done I must undo, come what might. This alien person from an unknown dimension had trusted me, and I had failed him. Not only my own honor rode upon my actions, but also that of my world.

I spoke into the fresh spring breeze. "Shreevalich klioth in halam narrettich praya. Shreenoloth kan cratanath prayanich halo. Korech liyat alla!"

The breeze stilled. The tiny sounds that had filled the moor quieted to utter silence. Carl's shape seemed frozen, unbreathing, where he stood. The light layer of cloud that had crossed the lowering sun's face moved no more.

My own body felt leaden, cold and without strength, as if every bit of energy it contained had been drawn away into the sword of Dorin Anthelles that rested on my icy palm. The blade was colder still, yet it seemed to vibrate. I almost expected it to rise of its own volition from my extended hand, to hang in midair.

The tension was unbearable. I felt my hair striving to crawl from its confining braids, my skin prickling into chill-bumps. The skin of my face seemed drawn too tightly upon my bones, making me grimace. Fear congealed in my belly, my heart, as I stood there, powerless to move, once the spell was spoken and the die cast.

If I had thought myself at that point to be under the utmost stress that nature might bear without reacting, I was wrong. It continued, and it grew. I felt almost levitated

from the hummock into the tense air, pulled and com-
pressed simultaneously by the forces that surrounded me.
One braid twitched on my shoulder, the only moving thing,
it seemed, in all the world.

It had to break, else I must break in its stead. For the
first time since I had found my growth, I was in the grip
of a thing that I could not control. My size could not help
me to conquer this. No blow to be struck, no spell to be
spoken might release me from this terrible thing that held
me, frozen, upon the moorland in the shadows of those
potent pylons.

There came a crack more forceful than thunder. A
spark ripped across the sky, coming from the northern
point to touch the tower to the southwest, then that to the
southeast. It returned to its source, making a triangle of
fire. Though nothing moved, there was a change in the
atmosphere. The tension was of a different kind, less pain-
ful, more positive.

The blade on my hand began to turn. Deliberately, it
spun from point to point, moving faster as it passed each
peak's position. It became a blur of light, reddened by the
light of the sun, which was now on the point of setting. Only
my long arm kept the whirling blade from slicing into my
flesh, for it was propelled by great power.

The sun reached the horizon. My heart sank. Would
all this be for nothing?

The blade slowed. I could see it, instead of a wheeling
blur. My hand began to grow warmer, as did the sword it
held. The thing moved more slowly still. And it stopped,

quivered, then steadied. The point was unequivocally directed toward the northeast. Toward he invisible mountains that lay, I knew from my old lessoning, over the shoulder of the moors.

My knees unlocked; my body went limp, and I fell, to sit on the greening turf. The blade chunked softly into the soil, gleaming in the last light of sunset, still pointing toward the northeast.

I shuddered. Though I had chosen to travel northward, I had not intended to venture into the mountains. There were tales told of those reaches of our continent that would curdle the blood of those who were neither over-young nor over-credulous. And they did not deal with the doings of men.

I moved one hand, with great effort, and drew the sword toward me. I set the spell-book on top of it, as carefully as if the fate of my world depended upon its being done just so and not otherwise. Then I looked toward Carl.

He had collapsed onto the turf, also. He was sitting with his knees drawn up, his invisible head in his hands. I knew that, as much as the spell had worn upon me, it must have been even more of a strain upon him, unused as he was to sorcery. I sighed and struggled to my feet.

He straightened, as my footsteps approached. I felt his unseen eyes on my face as I stood over him.

"The thing is done," I said, reaching down to help him rise. "I know now in which direction to seek our sorcerer, our adept. Not a Visionary, of course. They never take themselves outside the haunts of men, for their work is to deal with the things that trouble our kind. I can only hope that this unseen power-monger is of the better sort. Black sorcerers are a plague upon the clean world."

He stood beside me, and I felt a difference within his mind. The confining limitations that had been a part of it had stretched, loosed much of their grip upon his thinking. The thing that had happened to him, as well as the thing that he had just seen done and experienced, had shattered those iron-clad preconceptions of his. Now he was one with whom one of my kind could reason and communicate.

"That . . . that is the sort of thing your adepts do . . . easily?" he asked, as we moved away toward the ship.

"I have been taught so. Only one true witch has fallen in my path, and she was an ill bit of work of the dark sort. Selfish, grasping, without principle or decency. The kind that would boil a babe in a pot to make herself young and strong again. Yet I have been taught, and my tutor was a learned man and a skilled one, that there are more than a few among the folk of Garetha who deal in magics with a firm and beneficent hand. And the Visionaries hold the truth of the past and of the future and of the present fully in view for all to see, if they will. There is no excuse except basic malice for one who takes the black route to power."

He sighed. I stumbled in the semi-darkness, and he caught at my elbow to steady me. Then he said, "I see that many things can alter between dimensions. I was wrong to doubt you, Grittel. I suppose that I deserve what happened. A head unused might as well disappear."

I laughed. "But you must admit that it is working

quite as well as it did when it could be seen. Some lessons can only be learned in difficult ways, I have found. If you could look into my heart, you would find that I may be suffering even more than you, for it is by my fault and my over-confidence that you are in this predicament. That is the hard lesson that I am learning from this. And it is a difficult one, for I have always felt myself to be equal to any task or any danger that I might encounter. To find that I overestimate my abilities and my strength is a bitter blow."

We trudged on in silence, after that, each of us wrapped in his own thoughts. As we drew near to the craft, light bloomed about it, and the three who had waited there came forward.

"That was incredible!" said Leah. "I never saw such a bolt of energy in my life, even in the fusion-chambers of the power-plants. The thunderclaps that followed it shook the ship, and all of us found our hair standing on end!"

"But it did the task needful," I answered her. I pointed toward the mountains. "I must go there to find our warlock. It may take some time, for the journey will be long, and I have not been in these lands before. Indeed, none of my kind has traveled here, and there are not even travelers' tales to guide me. It was mapped once, so long ago that none now knows how or why; yet the maps show only the outlines of the coast beyond the mountains, and the ranges themselves, and these moors. It pains me to ask you to wait patiently for an unnamed span of time for an uncertain outcome, but that is all that I can do."

"We grow very patient in our sort of work," Anna said. "Those who aren't able are not chosen for it. Waiting is the thing we do for most of our professional lives."

"But not this time," said Carl. "Not, at least, for me. It is my head that is at stake, and I intend to go with Grittel to find the one who can restore it. Though I was never very fond of my looks, now that I can't see them, I find them acceptable. And besides, I can't shave, this way, and the stubble is driving me wild, already. It will cut down on the length of time if I am there at hand when she finds her sorcerer."

I had not thought of that, but it was completely logical. "I will welcome your company, and it may be that two may go where one could not succeed in going," I said to him. "I have no idea what we will find on the far edges of the moors, and even less notion what the mountains may hold. The tales I heard in my youth speak of dreadful creatures that live there. Dangerous beasts and things like men yet inimical to them. But two should be enough. More might well be a hindrance, rather than a help."

The three others had shown no great desire to go with us on our quest, and they heaved a three-way sigh of relief at my words, then began to busy themselves with supplying Carl's wants upon the trek.

Leah came down the ladder with a long tube, like the one that had been directed toward me on my approach. I looked it over as Carl slipped it into a carrying-sling.

"But will that thing work here?" I asked him. "If your craft will not operate, do you think that thing will?"

He took it from the sling and held it in the crook of

his arm. A clump of stone lay at some distance; he pointed the thing there and pressed a button on its side. Nothing happened. He checked it over, replacing a cylinder that was snapped to the underside of it, then tried it again. Still nothing.

"I thought as much," I said. "Probably not one thing that is a part of your peculiar system of power will operate here. So it is just as well to save carrying the weight of something that will be useless. Have you a long blade of any kind? Or even a metal rod that might serve as a knobstick? I have found that to be a most serviceable weapon, in my journeyings."

An arm-length rod with nubbled attachment at one end was found. I looked at it closely. "Ah, it is like the gears on the wheels with which we grind grains and tala seeds!" I said.

Wolfert came to my side. "You use the wheel? And gears? Levers, too, probably. Things that convert and apply physical force?"

"Of course. It saves much labor and does far more work. These things work in your dimension also, I take it."

"Hmmm." He rubbed his chin. "Basic physical things we have in common. It's just the more—sophisticated?—kinds of power that are different. Interesting . . ."

Carl straightened from tightening the straps of his pack. "We haven't time for a seminar in comparative physics," he said. "Not if I want to get back my head. We need to get some rest, so we can start early in the morning. I'm about shot, and I should think that Grittel would be, too. If that spell drained me, what must it have done to her?"

Then the weariness hit me. Scarcely waiting to eat a bit of the stuff from my pack (we had doubts about the effect their food might have on my system), I rolled myself in my sheepskin and stretched on the floor, while they went to their bunks. My last waking thought was a vision of flashing bolts, zipping across the space of the moor, linking purple-black pylons. I wrenched my mind from that and slept.

X

ThE MOUNTAINS of MYRThiON

We set out early. All the other travelers rose to see us off, and Carl turned more than once to look back as we moved away through the ground-mist. The lights of the ship became blurs of brightness, then ghosts of blurs. Once they disappeared into the dimness he steadied in his pace, and we went on, wordless, toward the northeast.

He had protested at leaving before light. "How will you keep on course?" he asked me.

His question had puzzled me mightily, until I sorted through his thoughts and realized that his kind had suppressed the instinctive part of their natures until the automatic direction-finding mechanisms of the body had been shut off. A strange thing. He had in a pouch of his suit a device that pointed always the same—to southward. By that he proposed to seek out our destination.

"I will know," I reassured him, as we took up our packs. "You might look over all of Garetha and never find one, young or old, who hasn't the ability to know with certainty the direction in which he is going."

I could feel him worrying about this as we moved carefully through the mists. He came, truly, of a skeptical breed. I had never known anyone who so fervently distrusted his own instincts as these outlanders did. I found myself wondering if the lives they made for themselves on those planets beyond the dimension-barrier were not uncomfortable in the extreme. Distrusting themselves, how could they ever trust one another? Or their own lawgivers and intercessors? It posed an interesting question, and I mulled it, as the sun rose and the mist melted away, and the moor fell behind us.

We reached the high point of the rise in the moor. Here it flowed downward again, only to swell upward even higher at the edge of vision. In the lowest part, away to our left, stood the pylon. Though it was miles from us, its dark shape made my skin quiver with a chilly shudder. Even Carl seemed fascinated by it, and he turned his gaze, now and then, toward it as we strode into the down slope of the moor.

Once we topped the farther swell, the sun was standing at noon. In the hard light, we looked across the last reaches of the moorland to see foothills rising at the horizon's edge. Beyond them again loomed a dim mass that I knew to be the outermost of the mountains that those unknown cartographers had named Myrthion. Then I shuddered in earnest.

"Can we make the foothills before dark?" Carl asked as we sat on the frosted turf that was just beginning to green a bit in these northern reaches where spring comes slowly.

I looked at the sun, down at that rolling line of hills. We had covered some miles since dawn, and another twenty or so lay between us and the nearest of the hills. I shrugged, looking down at Carl, who was panting with exertion.

"I am used to walking all day, every day. My long legs could make it before full darkness, but you are not conditioned to such heavy usage. Your legs are shorter. It will be with you; if you feel that you are able to try to reach the hills, we will. If not, we may camp there." I pointed, and he strained to see the darker spot I had noticed that marked a grove of stunted trees.

"I think I can make it. We work out regularly on the equipment in the gym of the ship. The air here's thinner than that I'm used to, that's all." Other than the panting, he seemed well.

"Then let us move." The two of us swung down the long reach that lay before us.

We approached the grove just before sunset. Even my legs were aching with effort by that time, for distances proved to be deceptive in the clear air of this higher country. By mutual consent, we turned into the trees.

It was much larger a grouping of woodlands than it had looked from afar. The trees were not the stunted kinds that the moors held, when they held any at all. Conifers mixed with big old hardwoods in a comfortable conglomeration that offered a choice of woods for fire-building. We took advantage of that at once, for the fickle spring was again flinging a fine mist of rain across the land.

We found a sheltered spot among young growth, whose needled thicknesses were as good as a wall against the wind. In the middle, we tramped out a clear spot and kindled our blaze. From his pack, Carl brought out a magically thin and tiny packet that opened out into a waterproof shelter large enough to cover both of us, and with that in place we found ourselves more comfortable than I would ever have thought possible.

As darkness wrapped us about, we heated rations at the edge of the fire, while the soft tick-tick of droplets moved among the greenery. Fearing to kindle more than we intended, we damped the blaze and banked its embers against need for a morning fire before we slept. The night crept very close then, and for some reason I missed the ruddy glow. I had never in my life feared darkness. But of course I had never before approached the Mountains of Myrthion in search of a wizard.

A sharp *crick* of sound woke me. I lay still, my ears questing for something more. In a moment another soft rustle among the young trees told me that something was moving toward us, and I jabbed Carl between the shoulder-blades with one finger. A cautious shifting of his length told me that he was also awake and listening. Satisfied, I drew my feet up silently, then sat in one noiseless motion. My hand was on my knobstick, which always lay alongside me when I slept in the open.

A snuffle, very quiet, told me that some beast was testing our scents. Though I had been familiar with all the creatures in the forests about Sundoth, I knew nothing of what might roam wild in these distant places. And as far as I knew, no other of my kind still lived who might have told me. A dew of sweat beaded my lip, and it had nothing to do with the chill of the night air or the dampness of the mist.

To make the situation worse, there was no light whatever. Thick layers of cloud covered the stars, and our fire was totally covered by ash and dirt. Perhaps embers still glowed in its heart, but no glimmer showed on the surface.

The snuffle became a low growl. Carl moved beside me. Silent as a serpent, he slipped away from my questing hand and was gone beneath the back part of the shelter. In my turn, I moved, feeling for the dry wood we had set at our feet in the enclosure in order to have it ready for the morrow. A couple of stubbled branches met my fingers, and I caught them up and stabbed them blindly into the banked fire, hoping that there was enough heat left in the coals to bring them to a blaze. Then I caught up my knobstick and turned to meet the rush of sound that now moved toward me.

I could hear breath, and I swung at the spot from which it seemed to come. My stick connected with a thud, and something was all over my feet. Furry, hot, stinking of something alien and frightening.

"Carl?" My voice was less calm than I might have wished, and I was extremely relieved to hear him answer.

"I got one!" he called from somewhere off to my right. "Did you?"

"I'm working with it now!" I said panting. My hands had, so far, grappled with two struggling limbs that seemed to have hands at their ends, but at least two more hands were trying to pull my feet from under me. I stamped hard with one heel and felt bone crunch. There came a howl from the thing.

The fire chose that moment to spark into life. It was only one feeble flicker, running up one of those dry branches, but it seemed to light the entire grove, after the complete blackness of a moment before. I could see the shelter, the nearer fronds of the circling bushes. I could see, once I found the courage to look down, a horrid beast-face staring up at me between the hairy arms that I was holding.

"Apes!" Carl was saying. "Big, ugly, hairy, but not, thank God, nearly as big as they grow on some worlds in our dimension."

"I never even heard a myth concerning anything like this," I said. "None of the Bestiaries list anything with four hands, a man's shape, and that—that terrible face."

Carl grunted and dropped his captive before the fire, which was now beginning to catch well. Before helping me with mine, he threw an armful of wood onto the blaze. Then we tied them both tightly and sat down to catch our breaths and decide what to do.

I could think of only one thing. "The book," I said. "I cannot believe that these . . . apes . . . belong here on Garetha. If they are constructs, there will be a spell in the book for making them, as well as one for unmaking them. Let me look . . ." I rummaged in my pack and took out the well-wrapped parcel.

In the uncertain light, it was difficult to see the crabbed

writing, but I struggled through a number of rather nasty formulae. And at last I found what I wanted.

"You'd better back away," I said to Carl. "I don't want anything else to happen to you, and I'm not at all certain exactly what this spell will do." He lost no time in adopting my suggestion, retreating into the shelter behind me.

I found the correct herbs and rubbed them onto the palms of those eight hands. Then I read out the ritual, there in the firelight with the light patter of mist falling onto the open book.

My gaze was fixed upon the page I was reading. I saw nothing until a gasp behind me caused me to glance downward. I almost gagged. The scruffy hair that covered the hides of the beasts was . . . melting. I tore my gaze from that, back to the book. Not until I finished the words did I look again.

The creatures were being unmade. Hide had dissolved into mud. Bones were rapidly becoming, once again, smooth rods of white wood, and the flesh that surrounded them had softened into a gloopy mess that charged the clean air of the grove with something awful.

I gulped. "There, you see? They *were* constructs. Their maker must have taken the shape from your mind. Certainly no person on Garetha ever dreamed of such beings as your apes."

"You mean he knows we're coming? And sent these things to stop us?"

"To stop us, perhaps. Or it might be that they were

simply sent to test us, try if we are bright enough and brave enough to be allowed to approach him. Wizards are strange people. No one really understands the workings of their minds. The one from whom I took the book delighted in the fact that she used neither logic nor justice."

"But he knew that we would come. That's what worries me."

I laughed. "No one ever crept, unsuspected, into the presence of a wizard. They know everything that concerns them, except for their own future. That is the one fact that saves things from disaster." He looked at me. I could feel his unseen eyes questioning.

"Witches and wizards are beings like ourselves. If they could see what is to come for themselves, they would work mightily to change the bad and to augment the good. And in so doing would probably disrupt the lives of the un-wizardly to a terrible degree. Besides which, it would be impossible to defeat one."

Carl sighed. In the fire-glimmer, I almost thought that I could see suggestions of his face as it caught the red light. I shook off the idea as simple wishing and poked up the flames.

"We should finish our sleep. Tomorrow will be more difficult than today, believe me, for we should get into the foothills. Unless there are wild beasts that wander them to make trails, the traveling will be hard. And I think that our wizard will let us be, for tonight, though I wonder what he may have in store for us as we come nearer to his home."

He scooped up ashes into a pile and distributed them over the blazing deadwood. I added handfuls of dirt until we had again covered it over. Without words, we stretched ourselves again in the shelter and pulled our blankets about our ears.

XI

STRANGE ALLY

The song of a brima woke me. For an instant I thought myself back in my room at Sundoth, listening to the winged singer carol his spring song in the tall oak outside my window. Then I opened my eyes to see the silvery sheen of the shelter above me. Carl's even breathing sounded from the other side of the enclosure, and I knew where I was and what must be done. I reached a long arm and touched him to wake him.

"We should eat well, so that we need not stop before nightfall," I said. "Can you bear to cook and eat with the stink of those things still in the air?"

He groaned; then he sat and sniffed. "Seems to have cleared away a bit," he observed. "And I'm hungry enough to eat, even if it hadn't. I'll strike the shelter if you'll build up the fire again."

Before the sun was more than a bright line along the

horizon, we were again on our way. The day looked to be fairer than the one before, for the cloud-layer was rolling away westward as the sun rose. The air was dried, filled with the soft scents that spring brings to northerly reaches of the lands. We stepped out strongly, and I found my spirits high, despite the eerie visitation of the night before.

Now we no longer moved across moorland. Patches of thorny scrub gave way to stands of graceful softwood that mixed their faintly greening branches with sturdy growths of juniper and low-growing pine. The land was rising rapidly, cut often by gullies and crossed by ridges whose backs were higher, each time we crested one.

At one such high-point, we looked out through a notch in the hills that now loomed close before us. Beyond that notch stood a peak, and I felt an ominous shiver along my bones to know that we stood so near those forbidding mountains. The sharp tooth was fairylike, its snows turned to silver by the sunlight. With my eyes fixed toward it, I set my feet to travel toward that notch, and Carl followed wordlessly.

The hills were rough, thickly grown with pine trees that gave way to fir as we crossed their expanse. There were game-trails, but they had been worn by hooves whose like I had never seen and paws of a size to give a traveler pause. Our first night there, we camped against an outcrop of stone with a fire before us that we took turns keeping ablaze. Wild voices called through the forest about us, and we had no idea what strange sort of beast might attack from the shadows beyond the light. But nothing troubled us, and we camped on the second night with more security of mind.

The next day saw the beginning of our climb into the steep lands, whose slopes were spiked with the tallest trees I had ever seen. Their boles were straight, rising cleanly from the needle-strewn mulch at the roots to a canopy of boughs that shut out most of the light from the sky. So steep was the footing, now, that we steadied ourselves against treetrunks, as we climbed, so as to avoid slipping down the declivities and coming to grief at the bottom.

We rested often, for the altitude was telling upon us both. As I caught and climbed and caught and climbed, my pack a pain of weight on my back, I found myself listening to my own panting breaths, then to Carl's—and then to those of still another. The laboring of a third set of lungs was clearly audible in the stillness of the wood. Holding onto a tree, I paused in the rhythm of my climbing and turned to look at Carl, who was some paces behind and below me.

"Do you hear?" I asked him.

He stopped, set his metal stick into the soil to hold him steady, and cocked his head, as I could tell from the angle of his shoulders. His warm cap rode eerily atop his invisible skull as he conned the still air of the slope. The other panting was still quite easy to hear.

"Somebody—or something—is behind us," he said. "I'll be damned if I can think what we can do about it on this steep place, though. Shall we go on?"

"It's all we can do," I replied. "But now that we know, we can keep a sharp watch to our rear. And once we find a spot to camp, we must be alert. Something tells me that we are not far from the wizard's lair; and if he is trying to halt us in our journey, then he must do it soon."

Weary as we were, we did our best to hurry, for neither of us wanted to be caught on that steep by night. Our only boon was the fact that no snow was left in these hills to make the way even less possible.

Before the light was entirely gone, we found a flat space at the foot of a tremendous scarp that went away out of sight above the tops of the trees. As I looked up at its dim expanse, I shook off the thought of what our journey might be like on the morrow. Tonight there was energy only for a fire, a meal, and rest.

With that impassable barrier at our backs, we felt a bit better. There was much deadfall lying under the firs, and the undersides of branches yielded dry underbark for kindling a fire. Upon these we piled dry sticks until they caught well, putting atop those the wetter and greener stuff we found and setting a pile of wet wood beside the fire to dry for future use.

"I can't see a wild animal attacking us past a big blaze," Carl said, as he sipped his concentrated soup and I chewed on my dried meat and fruit. "But if it's another of those constructs, you can't tell what an artificial thing might do. No instincts, if you take my meaning."

I thought it over as I chewed. "True. There are no rules of conduct that you can depend upon its having. I hadn't thought of it in that way, but you're quite correct. A fire might or might not have an effect upon such a creature. Still, we must have sleep. You sleep while I watch.

Then I'll wake you to take a turn while I rest. It's the best we can do, under the circumstances."

I could see him wanting to protest at resting first, but his shorter legs and arms had made much harder work of our climb, and he knew it as well as I. With a grunt, he rolled into his blankets, while I sat with my back to him, staring out across the fire at the trees that slanted abruptly downward from the edge of our resting-place.

That was a mistake, as I soon realized. The brightness made the shadows all but impenetrable. I sat for a space with my eyes closed, to allow them to adjust to the darkness. Then I kept them roving among the shadows that flittered about the perimeter of the firelight.

I was weary. It was difficult to make my senses follow the investigations of my gaze, and I often found myself dozing, wide-eyed. After one such bout, I came to myself to find that I was staring straight into two crimson eyes whose body must be just beyond the range of the firelight. Only the reflective eyes were casting my own light back toward me. I stiffened, my hand on my knobstick.

Yet the thing, whatever it was, was not moving. There was, in some subtle way, no threat to be read in those fire-colored orbs. It was watching me as cautiously as I watched it. I felt a pull at my mind, the faintest possible tweak. All sleepiness left me, as I focused on the unseen entity in the shadows.

I reached backward with my left hand and touched Carl's toe. His breathing changed. Then he moaned, "What's the matter?"

"Something is watching us," I breathed. "I can't see anything but eyes. Still, there isn't anything of the feel that those snuffles in the brush gave me. See what you think of it."

He moved to sit beside me. The creature didn't stir at his motion but seemed only to watch with interest. For what seemed a very long time we sat, examining our watcher while it examined us.

At last, Carl shook himself and said, "It isn't going to attack us. I don't get that feeling from it at all. Maybe if I went toward it, it would do something. We can't sit here eyeball-to-eyeball all night."

I nodded, and he eased forward, moving from a squat into a crouch, then standing upright in the rosy light. The effect of his missing head, in those particular circumstances, was eerie. But it had no effect upon those red eyes. They only seemed more intent as he walked toward the end of the ledge on which the thing must be sitting.

I heard his impulse in my mind before he opened his lips. Its connotations came to me, as he called, "Here, kitty-kitty!" in a falsetto voice. I almost laughed aloud.

But the thing came, and it was no kitty—not in his terms or in my own. An uglier beast I had never seen. Yet about its ugliness there was no sense of sickness and horror, as there had been with the apes. It was *humorously* ugly. Its round snout was covered with fine, plushlike fur. Its crimson eyes were also round and held an expression of innocent bewilderment. The podgy body was big, fully as large as a fair-sized dog. Unlike a dog's body, however, it was plump and soft-looking, as if a child's stuffed toy had suddenly assumed life. The fur on the body was a bit longer and softer and fluffier than that on the snout. The big mouth went all the way around from one side of the snout to the other, and its ends curled upward as if it were smiling. But the crowning touch of humor was its tail.

I laughed aloud at my first glimpse of that tail. It was not long. It began as if it were going to be smooth and normal, like that of a cat. A finger's length from its root, the thing developed a series of lumps, each one of which was tufted with long swatches of fur much lighter than that of its body. At the end hung a dejected tassel, much like that of a cow's tail. When the tail moved up, the tassel drooped. When the tail dropped, the tassel twitched nervously. And when the tail waggled sidewise, the tassel tried to stay motionless. A less likely tail I had never seen in my life.

Carl backed toward me, calling softly all the time, and the creature followed him sedately. Once Carl was sitting again beside the fire, it draped that tail across a stone and sat, catlike, with its paws neatly together, still regarding us steadily.

"It's got to be a construct," I said. "But what wizard would make such a thing?"

"A baby wizard," Carl said, his voice quite serious. "A very young one that found the ingredients in its . . . father's . . . toolbox or whatever, had heard the words spoken or seen the passes made, and decided to construct one for himself. Look at it! Who but a child could imagine such a thing—and then make it funny instead of frightening?"

I looked. Until we found a better answer, I decided that Carl's would suffice. The creature looked back at me, its red eyes winking in the flicker of the fire, and I could have sworn that it grinned at me.

Something niggled at the back of my mind. "You don't suppose—would a wizard make something like this to put us off our guard? Have it infiltrate us, so to speak? And then grab us when we are unaware?"

Carl shook his head. "Not with those eyes," he said.

I looked into the eyes again. No wizard that I had ever heard of could have done such a perfect counterfeiting of innocence. Not to mention bewilderment.

"We'll call it Beauty," I said, and Carl collapsed against my shoulder, whooping.

As if being named assured her of acceptance to our company, Beauty gave a delicate yowp, flicked his (her or its) tail around behind it, and curled up beside the fire. Carl shrugged. "I take it we can go back to sleep now. You, too, I think. I suspect that beastie will make an excellent watchdog."

If I could have seen his face, I'd have stared into it. "You think we can trust it, then?"

"Well, you're the expert on magics. But the job you did on my head seems to have given me more insights than I ever had before, and I say that we can both get a good night's rest while Beauty"—he almost choked on a chuckle—"keeps guard."

The strange creature raised its head and blinked its red eyes. That awful tail tried to waggle and was defeated by the even-more-awful tassel. It opened its huge mouth. I could see a double-row of serrated teeth glint in the firelight.

From that awesome orifice came the gentlest sound imaginable. "Yeep?" said Beauty.

I gave up and went to sleep.

XII

THROUGH THE HAUNTED HILLS

Between the foothills and the high ranges of Myrthion lay a wide belt of heavily-wooded country that was cut into gorges by streams running down from the snows. As we stood atop the last of the hills that we had conquered, we could see glimpses of falls amid the needled branches of the forest. The steeps that we had left behind us seemed tame compared to those that waited ahead, but we refused to hesitate at this point. Beauty in the lead, Carl following her, we set off into the broken country.

The forest here was of fir, and the damp from the many rivulets caused tufts of gray-green moss to fringe the branches of even the largest of the trees. Once into that dank dimness, we found ourselves smeared with green where we touched stone or twig or the soil itself.

We were following a path, though I could not determine in the spongy mulch what sort of track it might be.

The thing twisted almost as crazily as that old path in An-Perria's wood, but here it went upward so sharply that at any one time I was unable to see both of my companions.

I found myself shivering. Though the day was not cold, the damp and the eerie light combined to set my nerves on edge. The sounds of the others' footfalls were muffled in the soft soil, but when they broke a dead twig or called back to me, or when Beauty gave vent to one of her unlikely comments, the sound was unbelievably weird. And then I began hearing sounds behind me.

In this slick steep country I had found my size to be a disadvantage, slowing me so that the others gradually drew ahead. I had not seen Carl for some time, though he spoke now and again to cheer me on. Every time, he sounded more distant, and I had been putting forth every effort to catch up to him when I became certain that some creature was now walking behind me.

Another Beauty? I did not think that. There was something unpleasant about the noises on the switchback trail below me. And I had the feeling that eyes observed my back, when the undergrowth thinned a bit.

The light was beginning to fail, though I knew that the sun was still well above the horizon. The thickness of the needled canopy of branches shut out much of the sky's brightness, and night would, I was certatin, be upon us a full hour or more before its appointed time. I had no wish to be caught by darkness upon this up-and-down path with an unknown prowling at my back.

"Carl!" I cried.

"Yo!" came back his voice, blurred with echoes that mixed with those from my own call.

"Look for a spot to camp. It will be dark soon, and we need to find dry wood. This damp needs to be dried from our clothing, else we will be ill. Can you see Beauty up ahead of you?"

"No . . . yes! She's coming back to meet me. Must have heard you call. I'll see if she understands me well enough to hunt out a good place to stop."

I scrambled on, uneasily aware that the occasional sounds behind were moving closer. But now I could see Carl, who stood upon a huge log and waved me forward.

"Beauty found a beauty of a place. Right behind this log. We'd never have seen it without her. Him? Whatever. You want me to give you a hand?"

Now I panted wearily up to the log and leaned against it. "Thank you, but I'll make it quite well. When you looked back, Carl, did you see . . . anything . . . behind me? On the back trail?"

The cap jerked around. I felt his gaze on me. "Like what?"

"Not, I think, another Beauty. Something that feels frightening, actually. Not like the constructs, either. Like nothing I've known, but still oddly familiar. I kept wanting to run as fast as I could, even though you cannot run up this slope if your life depends upon it."

His hands went into his pockets with a nervous jerk. "I thought I saw something move. It might have been a small animal, disturbed by our passing. Just a blur of motion, nothing more. I hope you are just spooked. After today's climb, we don't need anything nasty following us. Or disturbing our rest."

"Thanks be for Beauty," I said.

He held out a hand and pulled me (with much help from me) onto the log. "There is the campsite we found. Couldn't be better . . . unless, of course, it was a cave."

The log on which we stood was only one of a tangle of fallen trees that must have been flattened by high winds. In the center of the mess was a flat space surrounded by tremendous ferns. Hornbeasts must have slept there often, for a clean trail led into it from downslope and away again, off toward the east. Plenty of dry dead wood lay about, under the outer layers of the logs. The space was big enough for a good fire, without endangering the ferns or the dead material that circled it.

Beauty sat amid the ferns, grinning up at us, her dreadful tail swishing enough to set the greenery swaying. I sighed and jumped down, followed by Carl. We soon had our packs unloaded and a fire begun. Yet all the while we worked, I could feel an unseen gaze prickling along my spine and at my elbows. Something was watching us from the tangle of growing things.

Carl felt it too. He kept looking at me sideways, as I could tell from the cock of his cap. Even from differing dimensions as we were, our races held the same atavistic knowledge of unseen eyes, looking.

We ate our scant supper in silence. I offered the pan to Beauty to lick, though I doubted that a construct needed food, or at least anything that I would recognize as food. She lapped it with gusto, however, and looked up at me to yeep for more. I took from my pack a lump of journey-bread, much hardened since leaving the Lady Dortha's hands. She took it into her big mouth with a glint of dagger-like teeth. After one chomp, she swung her head, flinging it into the air. She caught it on the way down and bit down hard. It crumbled between her jaws; she grinned at me as she licked the crumbs off her whiskers and chin and looked about to find any that might have fallen to the ground.

"I've learned something else about constructs," I said to Carl. "They *do* eat. Theoretically, they're not supposed to. At least, according to An-Perria's spellbook. Every day there seems to be a new lesson. One day, if I live so long, I may turn into a competent witch."

He sighed gustily. "How about right now? Something is moving the ferns down there . . . see?" He stretched his arm, and I sighted down it into the cuplike depression between the roots of two huge conifers. Something was there, for the ferns swayed with its passing. A few even broke, their stems hanging at an angle. The movement went into a thick clump and stopped.

I looked at Carl, and I could feel his unseen eyes shooting questions at me. I turned my gaze toward the fern-glade again. There was something about that invisible presence below us. Something . . . familiar?

I closed my eyes and let myself relax completely. My consciousness floated lazily in an eddy of memory. Dream-like, the sensations swirled about me, but there was also a sense of purposefulness. A voice rose from the deeps of my mind.

"His true name is Azatoth."

Ah! A demon? Or *the* demon, the only one that I had ever seen with my own eyes. Surely Dorin Anthelles was no sorcerer, to send his familiar after me so far into the unknown. The scavengers that he had set on my track were the limit of his imagination, I felt certain.

I had quelled that demon that its master had called Jereel. What happened to demons that were bested by mortals? I had no idea, but perhaps they were discharged by their disappointed masters. Or punished by whatever sorcerous power had created them in the beginning. Could that presence in the ferns be, indeed, that very demon that I had bested? Sent to do better this time? There might be a way to determine that.

"Carl," I said. He jerked and his shoulders turned toward me.

"Below there, that's no animal. It is—I'd take my oath upon it—a demon. I have met such before. In fact, I believe that this one may be the selfsame spirit I mastered in a struggle for power many months ago. If I can make it appear, I will know. Don't . . . don't be alarmed. They are all very ugly."

"A *demon*?" His voice was quiet, but I could hear negation all through its soft tones. "You want me to believe that there's a real . . . live . . . *demon* on our trail? I've swallowed a lot, Grittel, since I made your acquaintance, but this is one morsel too much. I cannot accept demons."

"Any more than you could accept the possibility of my . . . clearing your head?"

There was a muffled snort beside me. I put my hand on his shoulder and pushed him down into the bracken. "Be still and watch. If it's my demon, I think it will respond to its nickname. I'm saving its true one against the chance of need."

I knelt in the little clearing we had made and looked back toward the glade. Nothing moved. I stood to my full height and called, "Jereel!" in my most stentorian tones.

There was a flutter of ferns. A minor upheaval of some sort. Then, in the clearest spot the glade afforded, a shape began to form.

Carl jumped to his feet and caught at my elbow. "Do you see THAT?" he bellowed into my ear. "That—that *thing* down there?"

I gazed at the creature that was taking shape. Greasy-gray coloring: that was the same. Warty snout with little horns just above the red eyes. Yes. It looked like my former enemy. Though, in truth, I had seen only the one. They might all look similar, for all I knew. Yet this one had appeared at the calling of its name. It must be Dorin's demon, unlikely as that might seem.

"Yes," I said to the man beside me. "That's Jereel. I'd better tell you his real name, in case anything happens to me. It's a protection of sorts. Oh, and remember always that it's only the demon you *fear* that can harm you. I found that out the hard way."

He was holding my hand, now. Very tightly. But he was not shaking, and I put that down to his credit. My own kind would, most of them, be quaking in their boots before something like this.

The nasty thing looked at us, its red eyes gleaming in the last of the daylight. Its lips pulled back to reveal snaggled teeth, and I heard its voice.

"Darkness is falling. Night is the time of my strength, Grittel Sundotha. I have followed your track since my release from punishment, and I travel far more swiftly than your kind can do. You made a bitter enemy when you whipped Dorin Anthelles. You made one even more bitter when you humiliated me. The Maker of Demons dislikes it when we fail at anything we are set to accomplish. I was beaten with fires and fears and frozen things when my Maker called me back to his side. I owe you long suffering and unrestful death!"

Well. At least, now I knew.

"What did he say?" asked Carl, who had not understood the rush of my own language that had poured from the thing.

So I told him. I could see incredulity in the set of his shoulders and the clench of his hands. But it was his right to know, for I had brought him to this place and his present condition. Without my intervention he would be, most certainly, still with his ship on the plain, unable to travel, true, yet safe from demons.

His hand swept up and caught the cap from his head, flinging it to the ground beside his boot.

"You mean to tell me . . . that you . . . have a personal enemy . . . who is a *demon*? That very creature that's looking up at us right now?"

"I did not set out to make him an enemy," I said, somewhat defensively. "It is not my practice to be cruel to anyone, even a demon. But it was overcome him or be frozen into paralysis to await the coming of Dorin Anthelles's henchmen. I would not have survived for long thereafter. And that would be the *best* of what came about when that lecher regained his senses."

"Okay, I'll take your word for it. But what do we do now? My head, you are aware, is at stake. Your sorcerer who lives ahead, if your calculations are true, is my only hope. Right? If we don't get to him, I'll go through my life known as the Headless Horseman. Right? If this demon manages to do away with you, I'm out of luck, right? So what do we *do*?"

I smiled at him, reassured. "Oh, we attack him. That kind is not used to being attacked, I assure you. All of his habits and instincts are aimed at the coercion of those whose terrors have already weakened and subdued them. Believe me, the demon breed is not used to dealing with people who do not fear them."

"Speak for yourself," he said gruffly.

"You are afraid? But you should *not* be. It is very doubtful that Jereel could affect you in any way. You are of alien flesh and a spirit so far removed from any he knows that you might as well be a rock or a tree. He probably does not recognize you as being of mortal kind at all. No, he has come after me. So now I will go after *him*.

"You remain here and tend the fire. Beauty will be some comfort to you, I am sure. I go to stalk a demon in a fern-glade!"

I sank back into the hollow, letting the undergrowth hide me from the demon's gaze. Carl sat, too, and poked a small branch into the flames.

"I hope you know what you're doing!" he growled, as I crawled along the lower log to the spot where the path entered our camping-place.

And, in very deed, so did I.

XIII

CONFRONTATION

I had already read everything in An-Perria's book that pertained to demons. That first encounter with Jereel had made me cautious. But I had already found one method of dealing with the things. It had worked once with this very specimen. Perhaps I was embarked upon a foolhardy venture, yet I could think of nothing more unnerving than having a journey stalked, every step, by such a being. Instant death would be preferable. It was a pity about Carl's head, true, but I had a feeling that the sorcerer whom we sought was keeping an eye on our endeavors. He had, after all, been responsible for the entrapment of Carl's ship.

"It is difficult to keep a secret from a wizard," said one scribbled notation in the ancient book I carried. I had no doubt that whatever witch had scrawled the observation had had personal and unhappy proof of that. Thus it seemed to me that the one we were seeking must know who we were and what our needs might be. I left Carl to his discretion as I crawled away into the ferns and vines.

The steep slant of the land made for difficult going, as I tried to hide my great bulk beneath the over-healthy growth of ferns. My downhill hand or knee would slither from under my weight, squishing into damp pockets of moss or decayed vegetation. Yet all was so soft, so dampish, so cushioned with fungus and deep mold that I went quietly, for all that. I had no idea what kind of ear the demon might have, but I was certain that I was not rousing its attention by that means.

I made an arc through the forest, swinging wide at a level with our campsite, then sliding silently down through the thicknesses of greenery until I could see the top of one of the trees that sheltered the demon just to my right and above. I managed, in fact, to intersect the line of his approach to his glade, for I found the trail of bent and broken ferns that Carl had observed in motion. I moved past that, down into the level just lower. Then I worked my way toward the spot where he stood between the two great tree-crowns.

My skin was crawling; a prickling brought the fine hairs upright, made the skin itself pull up into ridges. Jereel was there; I could tell.

I felt eyes upon me, though I could see nothing in any direction. Then I knew that surprise would not serve me. It was as difficult to keep a secret from a demon as from a wizard. So I stood to my full height, which brought my face level with the spot where the thing waited.

It had gone invisible again, yet I could tell exactly where it stood. Something in me had waked fully, in the time since I had last met the creature, and it knew his presence instantly and infallibly. It also knew his power and his wickedness, which had not been true before, when I faced the demon in the strength of ignorance.

If I shuddered within myself, be sure that it did not show on the surface of my body or in my thought. Those red eyes were boring into me from very nearby. That ugly mouth was curling with contempt for the rash mortal who was thinking to contend with it.

I looked into those eyes, which could be felt so plainly. "Azatoth!" I said.

There was an unholy cackle of laughter. My skin bunched tighter.

"Do you think that the Maker of Demons is so unskilled that he would leave my name the same, after a mortal had discovered it?" he sneered.

I could feel tentative fingers of chill mist probing me, though they were invisible to the eye. A trace of that paralyzing aura that I remembered from Dorin's torture chamber was thickening in the air about me.

"It is only the demon you FEAR!" I told myself. My hands were steady, as were my knees.

I closed my eyes and thought deeply, sifting through the things that I had memorized from the spell-book. My hand clenched about the sprig of Solomon's seal that I kept in my pocket. The crisp feel of the dried stuff seemed to sharpen my senses.

The air was changing color, and not only because the

light had gone from the sky. The dim twilight was turning rosy, as if some hidden fire were showing through a fog. The probings at my mind, my courage were growing stronger, shaking me with cold, now. I crushed the herb between fingers almost too chilled to feel it, and its faint aroma filled the air. I caught my breath, relaxed by the tiniest degree.

There had been a spell in that book. For Joining with the Source had been the title written above the directions. I had wondered at it, what it might mean, as well as what source one might want to join with. Now I had a strong feeling that it was a source of good things. The page had been clean, and the writing disciplined and precise, not the crabbed scribbles of so many other spells.

I could no longer feel my feet. It might well be that Jereel would freeze me to this spot for eternity. Or singe me to ash. Or bear away my spirit to places I did not want to see or know of. I could feel the bond between spirit and flesh thinning. My lack of fear was helping a little, but there was so much power channeled through the demon that no lack of fear could divert its will from me. And I did not know its name!

The glade was now filled with smoky glare, as well as a subtle stench that I could not identify. Both were aimed at dimming my mind, subduing my will. I pinched a bit of the crumbled herb between numbed fingers and struggled to lift it to my lips. My hand was heavy as stone, my arm leaden. Inch by inch I forced the reluctant parts of me to move, to obey me, and the hand rose to my belt, my ribs, my shoulder. I laid the pinch of stuff on my tongue and swallowed. A jolt of energy shook me.

Something touched my elbow, and I started. Turning my head with difficulty, I saw a darkness there, displacing the reddish light.

"Grittel?" Carl's voice came from the shadowed shape. "I couldn't stay there. You need help. I can feel it."

Ah. Being unsubjected to the laws of our world, he was untouched by the demon's spells. And it might well be that I had need of him, if I succeeded in the thing I now felt that I must do.

"Carl. Help . . . me. Going . . . into . . . trance, I . . . think. Hold . . . me . . . up. Don't let . . . me . . . fall."

I felt his arm go about my waist, the jut of his shoulder beneath my armpit. He was no match for my height, but he was strong, and that was very good.

I closed my eyes and remembered the spell. For joining with the source.

The words were there, written upon my mind in the act of reading them, though I had made no effort to memorize them as I had so many others. I read them as if they were inscribed inside my eyelids.

"Eehren sentatens num pillebis ahroen. Uhm nokeles pelles tantat turtuis alom. Fisseburont pellant. Fisseburont sentant. Keleoens fahrante." The words moved upon my tongue and lips with a strangely soothing effect. I could only hope that the tiny trace of Solomon's seal I had swallowed would suffice for empowering them.

I could feel the steadying warmth of Carl's presence.

I could hear his breath, the separate beatings of his heart. I could feel the voracious self of the demon, as it strained toward me. But I was no longer quite where I had been. My self had moved somewhat apart from the tall body that Carl supported with his stubborn strength.

I could see the demon, quite suddenly, though he seemed unaware of it. He was straining toward the spot where my physical self was standing. Twin beams of scarlet shot from his eyes, bathing the body there in their light. The wide lips were curled back to reveal twin rows of saw-edged teeth that were gritted with concentration.

Carl was invisible to me, in whatever dimension I now existed.

Then I was snatched away as if by some irresistible wind. I seemed to be sucked up a white tunnel of force so powerful that it tore at the cohesiveness of whatever self I still possessed. Did I move between dimensions? Between worlds? I cannot say, even now. But when the pulling eased, I hung in a place that was not really a place as I had ever known it. It was so calm that one could not imagine any troubling of its peace, so filled with light that darkness seemed only an evil dream. In the first moment of my presence there, I rested totally from the trials and efforts of the months past. The stresses of my life were erased from me, washed away in the static flood of light.

XIV

THE SOURCE

For all the restfulness of the place in which I found myself, it also contained an invigorating energy. Nothing moved that I could see or feel, though I must admit that I had no equipment for doing either. I perceived, is perhaps the best way of describing the phenomenon.

There were currents of invisible, intangible force pooled and pulsing in that space, however. I felt my "self" pulled into an eddy, swirled about the area, lapped with— something. Thought? Knowledge? Understanding? Something of all those, yet like none of them.

I noted that there were areas from which my own eddy excluded me. It was as if I were supposed only to absorb a certain area of the atmosphere here. And I was absorbing it, I realized. I was soaking in great batches of comprehension. I understood, quite suddenly, the working of Carl's mind; and I realized that in this place, to whatever powered or motivated it, his dimension was as visible as was my own. As if this might be a central hub, from which all the varying dimensions rayed out in their infinite variety.

The eddy swirled. And I was suddenly faced with the reality of demons. The dark and mordant humor of the Master of Demons impinged upon me for an instant. The almost comical physical ugliness of the creatures. The trivial wickednesses that they abetted. They were amusing more than frightening, I realized. Their precious names were keys to their inner beings.

I projected a thought into the space about me. Jereel! Jereel?

The image of the creature appeared in my mind, clearly and precisely. And above it hung a haze of blue that drifted away, in a moment, to surround me. Within it was the name. Keshtath. His new name. The key to unlocking the force that he was exerting upon my helpless body . . . back there.

The eddy was moving me away from the central pool, now. Toward the place from which I had come. I resisted, for I desperately wanted to swim through that sea of knowing. To understand all the realities of all the universes, all the dimensions, all the kinds and forms of living things whose matrices must be locked into this cauldron of central creation.

Now I understood what was meant by the source. I also understood why it was a thing unvisited by those who worked the dark practices. To understand all is to undergo all. And who would choose to suffer with his or her own victims the things of pain and terror devised by his own mind and hands?

I wished that I could have found the reality of the sorcerer we sought. Of Beauty, whatever that odd creature might be. But I was placed back on the single point of solidity from which I had been taken.

The return was swift. I found myself standing in the red mist, Carl's shoulder still rock-steady beneath my armpit. I opened my eyes and straightened my back.

"Fine, now," I said, my voice coming with some difficulty. "Got what we needed. Hold steady for just a little more."

His grasp relaxed, but I felt his warm presence beside me, as I turned my eyes toward the demon.

"Keshtath! Return yet again to your maker. And know that I understand, now, what you are. Why you are. You and your kind are a joke played upon mankind by a warped humorist. If I should see you again, I might well laugh aloud—and that, as you know quite well, would shatter the particles that form you into nothingness. Pursue the ignorant, if you must, but be prepared for a day when even they learn to laugh at your posturings and your posings.

"Go!"

The mist faded. The red eyes glared into mine, but their spell was snapped totally. The demon faded to a chill blue. Then he was gone. and night filled the small glade.

Beside me, Carl's breath went out of him in a long whoosh!

"If we climb straight up, we'll reach our camp," I

said to him. "You can see the firelight on the treetops from here."

Without a word, he followed me up the steep slope, over the log that formed the downhill wall of our camping place. The ruddy flicker of coals was unable to warm the pallor of his hands, and I knew that his invisible face would be as pale. I reached for our pile of dry wood and put more on the burned-down heap of coals.

"Get warm. I'll put on the pot and make our meal. That was enough to pull the strength from a stone!" I said, and he made no protest.

When the dried meat was simmering in a broth with the herbs I had gathered as I moved through the forest, he relaxed a bit. I could see from the angle of his cap that he was full of questions, but I put them off until we both had eaten and were warm.

Then they came. "That . . . was . . . a . . . real . . . demon." This was no question, but a sober statement of fact. I nodded.

"It almost got you. I could tell when I touched you that you were almost gone. What did you do?"

"I used a spell from my book. For Joining with the Source. I didn't know what it would lead to, what source I might find myself joined with, but there was nothing else to do at that moment. If he had subdued me, he might have noticed you. And you had no weapons for battling such as he."

"That's for damn sure," he grunted.

"What was it you said to him, there at the end? After

you came back from wherever you went? I don't understand much of your language."

I laughed and told him. He thought it over for a long time.

"He was a mean joke. A wicked one. Just as Beauty is a happy joke, and a kind one." His voice was thoughtful. At his words, Beauty moved from the spot where she had been sleeping beneath the ferns and nudged his hand with her snubbed nose. He patted her absent-mindedly.

"Nobody sent him after you this time? The man you told me about, the one you whipped, he didn't?"

"Oh, no. Dorin wouldn't have thought of such a thing. No, Jereel's pride was damaged. He was punished by the jokester who made him, so he swore his own revenge. It's not common, but I've heard of such things."

"And this time, he should be gone for good?"

I patted Carl's shoulder. "He won't dare risk being destroyed. And I learned, there at the source, that heartfelt laughter can blow him to atoms. That's why the maker made his creations so fearfully ugly; nobody who looked at one could possibly laugh at it. They all look wicked and cruel and dangerous. But now we know."

"Then, if it's all right with you, I think I'll turn in. I wasn't about to go to sleep until I was sure that thing wouldn't come back."

My long shanks were aching with the climb, the stresses, and the weariness of travel. "That sounds like the thing to do," I replied, and we covered the fire and rolled into our blankets.

XV

THE LONG WAY DOWN

We woke, next morning, feeling cramped and sore and grumpy. I knew when my eyes opened that I was going to pay for the previous evening's entertainment. As soon as Carl's capped and invisible head rose from his sleeping roll, I understood that even he had been touched by the stresses of removing the demon from our track. The cap was pulled forward, its central button cocked at an ill-tempered angle.

"Do we ever get out of these damned mountains?" His voice was as ill-tempered as his cap.

I groaned and sat up. My braids were in wild disorder, and I sighed and grubbed in my pack after my brush.

"Women!" snorted Carl. He shoved some branches into the buried heap of coals from the night's fire, and after a moment a thin crackle of flame and a thread of smoke rose into the still morning air.

Ignoring him, I brushed out my undistinguished hair, braided it tightly, and set myself in order before retiring into the bushes in the opposite direction from that Carl had chosen. By the time I returned, the fire was burning well, and he had the pot of water pushed into the edge to heat.

Once we had washed and replaced the dirtied water with fresh, we both felt more nearly like reasonable beings. Without any unnecessary words, we made our thrifty breakfast, damped down the fire carefully, and made up our packs.

Beauty had retired into the ferns while our ill tempers were in evidence. She bounced back onto the path ahead of Carl, however, as soon as we left the camp. Her dejected tail belied the happy springing of her steps as she moved up the steep, switchbacked trail, leading us as rapidly as we could manage the climb. She seemed to know what lay ahead and to be excited at the prospect of reaching it.

Needless to say, I fell behind again. Moving my bulk almost straight up for long periods at a time becomes very tiring. The morning was half-spent when I heard a hail from Carl, who had made a better task of keeping up with our guide.

"I'm coming!" I called, rather crossly. I was out of breath, my pack was binding my shoulder, and I had a stone in my boot. But I hurried, nevertheless, to reach the level at which he had evidently stopped.

He was standing beside Beauty atop a knife-edged

ridge. The last, the topmost point before the falling-away of the slopes on the other side of the range. Other heights lay before us, but not in the unbroken mass that had met us from the other side. A cut that was doubtless the course of a river made a wide gash through the tangle of slopes and valleys and heights ahead. It led in the direction I had determined upon as that to follow.

"Well," I said, stopping and sitting on a nub of rock protruding from the bones of the mountain. "We seem to have come to the top. It shouldn't be terribly far, now. I feel something like a tingle or a hum; can you feel it?"

The cap cocked onto one side. I could see almost as well as if it had been there the twist of his mouth as he strained his perceptions after the thing I meant. I knew he had not found it when the cap leveled again, and the shoulders drooped.

"Not a trace. You think you're getting some signal from this sorcerer?"

"Or from his surroundings: his tools, his existing spells, or even his associates. Something is giving me a guiding. Aside from Beauty. See! She wants to go that way, too."

The construct was gazing off into the distance. The tail was attempting a wag, but it was only achieving a half-hearted waggle at its latter end. The busy stub and the three hairy lumps were moving madly, though. She could not have said it more plainly with human speech, "There! That's the way to go! Why don't you both get up and come, right now?"

But the slope up had taken much of my energy. I needed food to restore me, and Carl was also ready for rest, though his smaller physique needed less stoking than did mine.

"Hold on, Beauty," he called to her. "We're going to rest a bit before we start down. You come on over here and lie down. You'll wag that thing you call a tail completely off, if you keep jerking it like that."

She heaved a sigh and trotted along the ridge to the wider spot we had found for opening out the packs and digging out dried meat and fruit. Those round eyes watched every move with interest as we ate. I held out a bit of the meat toward her. She sniffed it and grinned, that huge, saw-toothed mouth managing to be friendly rather than frightening. Then she chomped her teeth into the morsel, chewed a moment, and swallowed noisily. And wanted more! I cut off another chunk and gave it to her. She took it between her paws and proceeded to nip off ladylike bits and munch them, while gazing dreamily across the prospect below.

I wondered quietly if a construct that became enough like a real, natural creature might not achieve its own kind of true reality. Why not? I rather hoped that that might be true, for I had no desire to see Beauty dissolve back into whatever strange components had made her.

Carl was thinking something similar, for he looked at her, then at me. He shrugged, and his cap cocked inquiringly toward me, but I shook my head. I didn't know, and there certainly wasn't anything in the spell-book about a construct that *ate food.*

We didn't linger for long. Once our legs had regained a bit of strength and we had repacked our supplies, we were ready to follow our unlikely guide down the angling animal trails that marked the steep slope at our feet. On this side, the mountain seemed to be mostly grassy land, the trees left behind us just on the other side of the last ridge. Droppings told us that this slope, steep as it was, must be heavily used by hornbeasts. And that told me another thing.

"Where the hornbeasts range, their predators also hunt. The wolock that prey on the smaller animals down in the southern forests are likely to have counterparts here. The beasts of the lowlands are big and fierce and dangerous, even to one of my size. Here, where they are provided every sort of game, plenty of room to roam, and freedom from those of mankind who keep their numbers down, they may be larger by far. Listen carefully, watch closely. We don't want to be surprised by any creature that may live here."

Carl grunted, and his cap cocked alertly. But it was past midday, warm on this protected slope. The sunlight was golden on the swaying grasses, and no sound but its gentle hissing came to our ears. The scent of the vegetation was pleasant, and there was no taint of any wild thing to trouble the nose.

We went downward carefully. On the wooded side of the mountain, there had been trees to break any fall, and we had been going upward. It is far different when you descend. The foot does not meet the ground with equal firmness. It is easier to trip and roll. With nothing save small shrubs to catch onto, a fall could send one of us into the invisible deeps that disappeared in sun-shimmer and shadow below.

Beauty was flowing down the slope, steep as it was, with such ease that I found it in my heart to envy her. She seemed to have an instinct for finding the easiest way, the most secure footing. I was lulled into trusting her guidance, and that proved to be folly.

The slope took on an even greater pitch, and at the line where a ledge of rock dropped away to the greater slant, Beauty stepped down onto a boulder that looked solid to the eye. Carl followed her, and it held his weight without protest. But when I set my bulk upon it, the thing tilted beneath my feet, throwing me off-balance. I rolled down-slope in a tumble of pack and elbows and flailing limbs, though I tried desperately to dig my hands into the scanty soil. Behind me, I could hear Carl's cry and Beauty's "Yeep!" Before me, I knew, was a drop into the river gorge. I didn't know how far that might be.

I was saved by a hole. Some big stone had evidently been torn from the mountainside at one time, leaving the cavity where it had rested waiting for my time of need. I tumbled into it in an unseemly heap, and beneath me I heard an ominous crack. One of my long legs had twisted as I fell, and a melon-sized rock at the bottom of the depression had finished the task. I knew that my left leg was broken below the knee.

Clawing at the pack-straps, I managed to remove the

burden from my back. This allowed me to straighten my spine, remove the worst of the grit and grass from my eyes, and survey the situation. The movement sent red-hot bars of agony down the leg.

"Grittel!" Carl's voice rang down the steep, and I could hear his concern all through the cry. Those who travel the sorts of roads we had together become more than merely companions. A kind of brotherhood develops, a bond of affection unlike any other.

"Here!" I shouted, as loudly as I could manage. "Watch your footing; I think I am not far from the edge of the gorge!"

There was a pat of paws above me, and I looked up to see Beauty's ugly face hanging over the edge of the hollow. "Yeep?" she asked anxiously.

"I'm not killed," I told her, as she leaped down to nose me about, then to sit staring at me with her round red eyes, as if she understood all that was implied by my broken bone.

Then Carl appeared, his cap bobbing above emptiness. "Okay?" he asked.

"Not precisely. I have broken my leg. On this slope a crutch would be—unfeasible. To carry me would be impossible. I am stuck here, I'm afraid."

He jumped down into the hollow and sat beside Beauty. His fingers explored the leg-bone quite gently. "Mmm. Clean break. Needs to be set before it swells. You game?"

I had learned his ways well. When he was truly concerned, he spoke in just such choppy phrases. I eased myself back against the curve of the dip, as he steadied the leg with both hands. When I looked at it, I knew that it must be straightened quickly, or I should walk awry all my days.

"Do it now," I gritted. "Use my knobstick to tie it straight. There are strips of cloth in my pack."

He dug into the pack, found the strips, then slipped the knobstick from its loops. "Steady your other foot against that rock," he said, pointing to an edge of stone that thrust through the floor of the hollow, and I obediently set my right boot-heel against it.

Beauty threw back her head and howled dolefully, as if she dreaded the pain that was to come. Then she pushed her big, warm, ungainly body into my arms, as if to say, "Hold onto me!"

I hugged her against me, and Carl caught my foot in both hands. When he tugged the leg straight, I almost squeezed Beauty into halves, but the bones clicked into alignment. Carl eased off a bit, to see if they would hold while he secured the stick to me. Seeing what he was doing, Beauty disengaged herself and went to sit beside my left foot, and when Carl laid the stick into place and began tying the strips, she caught my boot in her mouth (so large was that mouth that my entire boot-foot fitted into it) and pulled gently to keep the leg straight.

Once the thing was immobilized, the pain subsided a bit. I needed water, for I had sweated away most of what I had drunk earlier, so Carl opened the bottle. Then, for lack of anything else to do, we ate a bit. That delayed the moment when we must look one another in the face (as much as could be done, under the circumstances) and ask the fatal question, "What now?"

Carl surprised me. When he had tidied the packs again, he sat beside me and put the spell-book into my hands. "There might be something in there that could help us," he said. His cap was at its most even and serious level, but I imagined that his invisible face might well be blushing at the thought of consulting witchcraft for a way out of a predicament.

I nodded and opened the book. "I am no adept, to transport us through the air," I said, as I turned the pages. "Even if such a spell should be here, I wouldn't dare to try it. After what happened to your head—we might end in the gorge down there, or impaled on one of those needle peaks. But I will look. Perhaps there is something."

And there was. For Sending a Message Afar, said the title. I looked up at my companions. I felt a foolish smile beginning to form on my face.

XVI

A CALL
FOR HELP

The sun was now low. We, being on the northern slopes of
the range and the year being yet young, were in shadow,
and chill was settling into the hollow where we rested. I
was cold with shock, as much as with the natural coolness,
and before I attempted any spell-work, Carl insisted that
we must have fire.

"But there isn't any wood!" I snapped, a bit crossly I
fear.

"Didn't you ever read any Westerns?" he asked. Then
he thought. "No, of course not. You haven't any West. I,
however, DID read Westerns, and I learned many things that
would have been lost to my race if they had not been preserved for us in the guise of entertainment." He laughed
aloud as he rose. "I'm off to get fuel. Be back in a shake."

"You can't go all the way back up to the top after
wood!" I called after him.

"Don't intend to!" he caroled.

I looked at Beauty. She almost shrugged. We waited together, as the warm light moved away across the highlands on the other side of the gorge, and the foreground disappeared in a wash of purple shadow.

In an incredibly short time, we heard Carl's steps returning. He sprang down beside us, his hands occupied with the corners of his tent-sheet.

"Behold, our fire!" he said, dumping out a pile of dried dung from the sloping pastures above us.

"Ugh!" I said. "That?"

"Don't be sniffy!" he answered. "Makes a fine fire. You just watch."

He scrambled about the hollow, setting aside most of his disgusting treasure, heaping a small amount in the center of the depression. The device he used for making fire worked, which was a blessing, for I was saving my strength for my calling-spell. To my utter astonishment, the dry gray chips caught easily, and a yellow-blue flame rose into the still air of our shelter. He fed more chips onto the pile as the blaze grew. Before full darkness was upon us, we had a merry fire to warm us from the night.

Hot broth was a comfort to my inward parts, and the aches from my fall eased a bit. Only the leg now was a trouble to me, and that mainly because it was so hard to move about. But Carl helped me to sit straight, arranging the book in my lap so I could read by the firelight. Then he and Beauty took their places on the other side of the fire and watched me expectantly.

I pinched together three heaps of dried herbs. The first heap I put upon my tongue. The second I sprinkled into the flames. The third I cast upward for the air to disperse. The scent of basil filled the hollow.

Then, bowing my head upon my two fists, I gazed into the blaze, focusing all my strength of will upon my effort. For this was no strangely worded spell. It was a matter of concentrated effort, of willing, and of strength. Radiating outward from every inch of my long body I sent a cry for help.

Energy drained from me in almost visible channels. My eyes grew bleary, my mind dulled. I was caught out of my concentration by a sound from Carl. A gasp—or more of a groan. Looking up at him, I saw that he was facing toward the uphill lip of the cup in which we sat.

My gaze followed his. A wolock grinned at me, its fanged mouth reddened by the firelight. Beyond its shoulder, eyes glinted green, and I could see still other shaggy heads behind. As I watched, a row of pointed snouts lined the edge of the depression.

I glanced back toward Carl and saw that his hand had closed over his metal rod. Beauty had opened her mouth to show all her multiple rows of teeth. It was that display, I felt, that had held the beasts off our backs for even so long as this. A jolt of panic went through me; and I stared, once more, into the flames. "Help!" my spirit cried into the distances. Then the world blurred, and I leaned backward against the wall of the hollow, feeling the book slip from my lap.

It took only a moment for me to regain control. I could hear the many-breathed pantings from the edge above, the careful inhalations of my two companions. My own heart thumped in my chest with rib-shaking force. I curled my fingers about a small stone, knowing that I could never dig my blade from my pack in time to use it well.

The things were gathering nerve to spring into the fire-lit camp. In more populous areas, such beasts would never have approached so near to a blaze, for they would know that people with weapons were near. Here they had no such experience. It was, most likely, the fire itself that had attracted them to us.

The leader drew its blue-black lips back, revealing the sharp teeth, as well as the prominent fangs. A guttural, "hugh!" came from its throat, and I could see the muscles of its shoulders gather for the spring.

I flung my stone with all the force I could muster, just as the thing launched itself into the air. The rock thunked into its side, sending it off-course so that it missed Carl, who had been its target. By the time it righted itself and faced the man, Carl was standing, rod in hand, ready to counter any move it made. But now another leaped—to freeze in midair.

A small shape stood at the lower end of our sheltering hollow. Pale hair rose untidily about a round face, whose large gray eyes were filled with mischief. Below the face was the prosaic cut of a child's nightgown. Bare feet stood firmly on the ground beneath its hem.

I felt my mouth drop open as Carl edged back cautiously from the suspended wolock. He turned slightly, and I knew that his invisible eyes were focused on the newcomer.

The child was so young that it was impossible to say whether it was a boy or a girl. Yet the impishness of those eyes suggested "small boy" as nothing else could have done. He grinned, deep dimples touching his cheeks.

"You *did* need help, didn't you?" he asked in a husky little voice. "A good thing I wasn't needed in the Spelling, or I wouldn't have heard you. Father didn't, and he is FAR more sensitive than I am." He surveyed us deliberately, taking in the ring of frozen wolock, the fire and its unorthodox pile of fuel, my long and disabled shape, and Carl's peculiar condition. When his eyes turned toward Beauty, he laughed and clicked his fingers together.

She rose and moved to rub her ugly head against his shoulder. "I see you found my pet," the child said. "Most people find her frightening, but Father said I had the right to make her as I chose to. And I like her just as she is. I knew when she disappeared that Father must have sent her to do some task for him. And he sent her to you—how odd!"

"Your father being the sorcerer who lives just to northeast of here, I take it." My voice came out more steadily than I would have thought. "I hope to have the chance to greet him and to thank him for Beauty's company."

"Beauty? I like that. I had named her Gnash, but that's too mean-sounding for her disposition. Beauty . . .

that is what I'll call her, too." He patted the podgy head again, then sat almost upon my feet, the hollow being very limited as to space.

Carl's cap cocked upward for a glance at the motionless wolock. Then he turned it back toward the child.

"And what do *we* call *you?*" he asked. His voice wasn't quite steady, either.

The pale eyes blinked. "Oh, I am Nollie. The Lord Oreon's youngest, you know." He sighed a bit dejectedly. "That's why I wasn't allowed to stay up for the Spelling. It isn't easy, being the youngest in the family. But it was lucky for you, just the same. That wolock would have eaten you and the rest would have gnawed your bones. They are very vicious beasts, hereabouts."

"Thank you very much. I had reached that conclusion just about the time you popped into sight. I take it that you did that by magic?" I was astonished. There was no trace of sarcasm in Carl's voice.

"Of course. Nobody but the untalented use mechanical means. *Everyone* who lives here in the mountains is talented, or they wouldn't survive for very long. You must have some talent—or she does!" He nodded toward me.

"I have a spell-book that seems to be teaching me talents I never knew I had," I said. "It allowed me to call. I didn't know exactly who I might be calling, but I had determined through a triangulation that a sorcerer lived somewhere near here. It was the only thing I could think of to do; and Carl was the one who suggested that I look into the book. There would be no getting to the bottom of the steep, here, with a broken leg. Not without breaking everything else in the proces."

A small warm hand was laid upon my unhurt leg. "You have done a triangulation? Wthout training in the Arcane Lore? Just by using a *spell-book*?" Nollie's tone was almost incredulous. "Father must meet you! Perhaps that is why he has done so many strong spells, lately. Did he bring you to him?"

"I seriously doubt it. A combination of odd occurrences brought me to the place where Carl's ship is stranded. An accident made his head invisible. Then it was obvious that we must find a sorcerer to put things right."

"His ship? He came from *out there*?" The hand was lifted to describe an arc toward the sky. "You mean Father really DID catch one?"

I looked across at Carl. His cap-button glowered back at me.

"He did, indeed," came the voice from his vacant face. "He snatched us from our lawful duties and put us into a place where our systems do not operate. We are totally helpless. My people are there, waiting for me to return with some news, some kind of hope that they will get back to our own dimension." I had never heard him speak so formally. I realized he was holding in his anger, feeling it unjust to vent it upon the child when it was the father who deserved it.

Nollie looked at him, his eyes wide with astonishment. "You didn't *want* to come? To see a new place that wasn't like any you'd ever dreamed of?" He sounded really curious. "Father wasn't truly certain that a dimension of the sort he posited was actually in existence. His divinings told him that it should be. Only an experiment, a really strong Spelling, could prove him right or wrong. And Agiswis made a bet with him: Father hates to lose a bet."

"How long ago was this?" I asked, suspecting the answer.

"Oh, long before I was born. They knew when they put down the markers that it must be a long-term bet. Father could only set the focus of the stones upon a tiny spot in that other place, you see. A ship had to happen into it, and that might have taken lifetimes. It was lucky the stones were already up; Grandfather used them for talking with other worlds in *this* dimension." He grinned, satisfied that he had made everything quite plain to us.

Carl's cap regarded me questioningly. I looked, in turn, at the child.

"How long can you keep the wolock motionless? It must be quite a strain on your energies."

He laughed. "I draw energy from your fire, the stars up there, the pressures on the rock inside the mountain. I don't give away my OWN." He looked at me with sudden concern. "Do you mean that you sent out that terribly strong call from inside *yourself*? I don't wonder that you look so weary!"

"You must remember that I am doing things without understanding how or why, blindly following instructions I don't really comprehend. Now I'm tired to the very death, my leg is broken, and I'm stuck here on the mountainside and cannot go up or go down. Have you any suggestion at all?"

Instead of an answer, he lifted me. Bodily. All my great bulk rose a half-inch from the ground I lay upon. Then he let me down again, quite gently.

"You *are* heavy," he said. "I could take him, I think," he nodded toward Carl, whose cap didn't look at all happy. "But not you. And certainly not the two of you. And as soon as I was gone, the beasts up there would eat up the other one who was left here. Which would be you. And Father will want to see you almost at once. Or sooner. It is a problem."

He looked up at the stars, tracing the positions of the Wheel and the Plow, which were now almost down out of sight beyond the edge of our hollow. "The Spelling will not be finished before dawn. It is better if we wait here. Father will get us all back home. You will see. He can do *anything*."

Somehow, I was not reassured. I had thought the same of my own father in the days when I was possessed of fewer than six summers. It had not taken a long while thereafter to learn that he was one of the world's incompetents. Still, there was no choice left in the matter. I had no wish to try combatting the wolock with spells and herbs and stones. I had an intuition that of the three, they believed only in the stones, and there were too few of those to stand off the entire pack.

"That sounds like sense," said Carl. "If you can keep that thing from falling on top of me, I'll stretch out on this side of the fire. You can share Grittel's blanket. And

Beauty can pick her own spot. I'm too tired to worry about things." He suited his actions to his words, rolling out his blanket and lying upon it, directly beneath the suspended wolock.

Nollie chuckled, a charming gurgle of amusement. "I do appreciate your trust," he said, "but I had better set him back up there. I should hate like anything for him to come down and eat you in your sleep."

The wolock rose silently into the air until he reached the level of the lip above. Then he was pushed backward to stand among his fellows, his paws still braced for the landing that would never come.

The child yawned. "You woke me up," he said, burrowing in beside me, as I arranged the blankets to cover us both. "I must admit that I'm pretty sleepy. Father will fix things in the morning. You will . . . see . . ." and his eyes closed.

I lay for a time, watching the fire die, the stars wheel above, Beauty's eyes burning redly in the glow of the coals. Something was speaking to me, but I couldn't understand its words.

XVII

THE LORD OREON

A sound from above woke me. The sky was alight with dawn, and the shapes of the wolock, still poised at the edge of the lip, were beginning to quiver. Something like growling was rising from their rank.

Nollie's warm little self was scrooched against my side, and I reached down and shook him gently.

"Nollie! Nollie—your spell is wearing thin. The wolock are getting loose!"

He wriggled, burrowing his fair head further beneath the blanket, and I shook him harder. He grunted crossly. Then his head popped out, and his big gray eyes regarded me with surprise.

"Where? Oh, I remember. You're Grittel. He's Carl. We're out on the mountainside, with the beasts. How lovely!"

"Not so lovely if they break loose from your spell and have us all for breakfast," I said, gesturing upward.

He glanced up. His eyes narrowed a tiny bit, and the group froze again into stillness. His merry grin encompassed me and the morning world.

"There. I think they'd run away now that the sun is rising, but it is just as well to be quite certain. That is the first lesson in the arcane. Never take a chance."

"If I had only known that," I said, folding the blanket and rolling it to fit into my pack, "Carl might still have a visible face. You would be safely at home in your bed. And my leg would, most likely, be unbroken. I have learned the hard way about meddling with things I don't understand."

He cocked his head thoughtfully. "Well, that is true, of course. But I cannot see that you did anything that you *knew* to be wrong. Father says that that is the principal consideration. A mistake can be made by the greatest adept ever to live. Deliberate folly is another thing entirely." His solemn little voice accorded oddly with the maturity of his manner and vocabulary.

"Your father does sound wise. He must have brought fine teachers for you. And that must have been difficult, here in this remote place."

"Oh, he teaches me himself. And my sisters and brothers. Except, of course, for those who are already grown up. They help him teach the rest of us."

"You have a large family, then?"

"Six of us who are still little. Four who are old enough to teach us. Two old enough to help Father with his work. They don't pay any attention to the ones as small as I am, though. They call me infant!" His tone was filled with contempt for such obvious dullness of wit.

I laughed. "And are all your sisters and brothers as well-trained as you?"

"Oh, better. They have had more time, you see. Father cannot abide waste of time, and he starts teaching us in the cradle. Or he started. Now that our mothers are all dead, there will be no more."

"Your mothers?" One mother per family being all that I had experienced, I was curious.

"Yes. You see, Agiswis and Thellar are the oldest. Their mother died when Thellar was born. Then Cleva, Nellone, Marshak, and Fastor had a mother, but she didn't like living so far away from the world and pined away. At least that is what Nurse told me. *Our* mother died of a spell-casting. Father never talks of it, but Nurse says it was the doing of a witch. Don't, for my sake, tell Father you are a witch, Grittel! He has a prejudice against them."

"That is understandable," I said. "The single one of the kind I have met did not make me love her, be sure. I"—I found myself laughing conspiratorially—"boiled her in her own pot!"

He gave an excited little crow of laughter. "Did you *truly*? Wasn't it terribly difficult? I should think that she'd have cursed you like anything!"

"Oh, she did. The bubbles rose purple and green and scarlet for quite a while. It is her spell-book that I took away with me. The one that got me into all this trouble."

"They are like that." His manner was so entirely adult and knowledgeable that I found myself having to steal quick looks at him to remind myself that he was, after all, only about five or six years old. But he had looked up again to see the sunlight touching the ridge above us.

It's time to call Father. Do wake Carl, while I get my wits together."

I tossed a pebble against Carl's outstretched hand. "Wake up! Nollie is about to call for reinforcements. We should pack up everything. I don't know what he'll do, but it's best to be prepared."

There was a groan from the huddle of blankets. Carl's shoulders heaved up, the vacancy above appearing particularly eery in the absence of his cap. He scrabbled about, found that headgear, and flapped it into place. It cocked upward toward the motionless wolock.

"He had to put another spell on them a bit ago," I said. "They were beginning to move and make sounds."

"Whoosh!" he wheezed. "I dreamed I was back in my cabin on the ship. Back where I belong, in my own dimension. Felt mighty good, too. Then I wake up to this." He waved a hand toward the wolock.

After putting the packs into order, he climbed gingerly out of the hollow on the downhill side. I took the opportunity, Nollie having gone into some kind of trance, to attend to personal needs, a matter of some difficulty with a broken leg. I was rebraiding my hair when the child opened his eyes.

"Father wasn't terribly happy at being called, after Spelling all night. But he said he'd be ready to attend to things shortly. We should all stay close, here in this dip.

Have your things in your hands, he said." The child looked down at his nightgown. "I do wish I had my breeches. It's uncomfortable to go about in your night-clothes in the daytime."

Carl's headgear popped into view on the lower side of our shelter. He climbed down into the hollow, and we instructed him in the disposition of the packs and himself. It wasn't hard to get close together. If the sorcerer had told us to spread apart, that might have posed a real problem.

We sat watching the light move on the peaks and ridges of high country that lay within our view. When our slope lay in full sunlight, Nollie released the prisoned beasts, and they backed away from their positions, muttering and growling, to run at full speed out of sight. We had not rekindled the fire, having no idea when our would-be host might decide to appear and take us elsewhere, but Carl kicked the remnants of the ash-heap apart with the heel of his boot.

Nollie leaned against me, still sleepy after his interrupted rest. I put my arm about him. Something inside me felt satisfied for the first time since I had cuddled my sisters, years and years ago.

Without warning, I found myself rising into the air, the child still held against me. Carl, too, was lifting, legs crossed, hands frozen about his pack and his iron rod. As a group, we were lifted above the level of the higher side of our dip, then higher still until we could see out over the river gorge, just below, and the high ground beyond it.

I shook Nollie. He opened his eyes, looked about, and

sighed with contentment. "I *told* you Father could attend to everything," he said. His head dropped against me again, and his eyes closed.

I could only hope that his sire deserved such unquestioning trust. I could tell from the tilt of Carl's cap that he, too, was concentrating all his energies toward helping our unseen host. His knuckles were perfectly white as they gripped his possessions. Mine would be, also, I knew; I refused to look down at my pack.

We rose higher into the air, made a swooping turn that made my stomach queasy, and arrowed off, following the gorge's windings. That was somewhat of a relief. I had had mental pictures of soaring full into one of those rocky bluffs.

Still, I reflected, Lord Oreon had taken much trouble with the education of his son. Had my first and only suitor done as well, I might even now be supervising the rearing of his brood. Surely paternal affection would not allow the sorcerer to endanger his youngest child.

The thought comforted me, and I yelled across the rush of wind to Carl, "He wouldn't chance hurting Nollie, would he?"

Carl's cap waggled a precise no. The sensation of seeing the stone cliffs rushing past between his collar and his cap did something odd to my stomach, and I closed my eyes and held onto my now-distant supper.

I felt us turning once again. The texture of the rushing air changed, becoming warmer, damper, less abrasive. I chanced a peep, and we were almost at ground level. A valley that was already green with spring, even so far north, lay a few yards below. The scent of blooming things reached me, as well as that of bruised grass and clean chimney-smoke. Hedgerows dashed past at blinding speed. A meadow, already knee-deep to the beasts grazing there. A garden . . . We slowed, hovered. The grassy sweep was closely mowed, its green patterned with gay flowerbeds. Our group came to rest in the center of that natural carpet, so gently that we hardly bruised a stalk of the grass.

I had closed my eyes again, just to get myself settled. Now I opened them to see a figure hurrying toward us across the lawn.

It had to be Nollie's father. The fair hair was tousled almost as badly as the boy's had been. The gray eyes were wide and concerned. The round face was as rosy as that of a grown male can become. He was not overly tall, slender as a blade, and he bent over Nollie and lifted him in his arms before he so much as greeted Carl or me.

"Lord Oreon?" I asked, loosing my fingers from my pack-straps with some difficulty. "Grittel Sundotha gives you thanks. Without your son's help, Carl and I would have made a meal for wolock."

He did look at me then. His color rose in his cheeks, as he realized that his manner had been wanting.

"Forgive me, Lady. This scamp has had me so concerned that I hardly know where I am or what I do. I am more than happy that he came at your call; but he will be given a talking-to, nevertheless. It would have been quite possible for him to call me, even in the midst of a Spelling."

But a wide grin belied the sternness of his words, and he beckoned to a pair of tall young men, who came forward and lifted me between them.

"Do allow us to take you into the house. You need rest and care, and I have no doubt that the both of you need food as well. Eh?" He hurried ahead to open the wide doors, and we were carried into the big stone farmhouse.

XVIII

A Family
of Magicians

There was no grandeur about Oreon's home; or, indeed, about his person or his children. The house was big. It was strongly built, warm and secure against the mountain blasts. It was pleasing to the senses in a comfortable way, and every bit of its furnishing and ornamentation was immediately usable or enjoyable. Pots of living blossoms scented its atmosphere with spice and sweetness.

I was laid upon a long settle in the big kitchen-sitting room. Bright cushions propped my head and shoulders, so that I could manage to eat handily, and the big pots of porridge on the hearth rivaled the Lady Dortha's own. I took the bowl that Nollie handed me and finished it off too quickly for good manners.

When I looked up from my meal, I found a self-possessed young woman watching me. She, too, was fair and not over-large. In a normal place she would have had every swain for leagues about making a road to her doorway; but when I looked more closely, I saw that she was in no sense as young as she appeared. Older than I by a double hand-span of years, I guessed. Her incisive glance, the set of her mature lips proved her a thoroughgoing adult.

She smiled at me and took the bowl. "I am Agiswis, Nollie's oldest sister. And you are Grittel. I am so glad that you have come at last."

At last? As she walked away toward the big stone sink, I mulled her words in my mind. When she returned, I looked into her eyes. They were deep, knowing, wise beyond measuring.

"At last?" I asked. "Is it, then, true that I have been brought, all unknowing, to this place?"

"Oh, no! At least, not in any sense that we forced any happening upon you. Yet Father knew on the day that you were born that a major talent had come into the world. He followed your rearing closely, and I must say that he totally disapproved of both your parents. It would not have been either wise or just to take you from them, however. And, though I wondered at that, once I grew old enough to realize who it was that he watched so closely in his scrying, now I know his reason. You came, Grittel, by your own unwarped instincts and choices."

"If he watched so closely, how is it that he did not know of our need for help on the mountainside?"

"A Spelling requires all energy, total attention. And that was a vital Spelling, indeed, for it brought a loop of that other dimension . . . from which he came"—she bobbed her head toward the place where porridge was disappearing into thin air between cap and collar—"into this one, so that their devices might operate to take them home to their own place. It was a long night's work, upon my soul, and one that I am happy to have done. Ill was the day that I placed that bet with my father!"

"You were able to look across that vast gap, into Carl's own?" I was astonished at the thought of such purposeful focus and control.

"Not so very amazing." She laughed. "It was not done blindly, silly girl! We had the focus already in place. Do you not remember the stone pillars? Their field has never been entirely in the here and now. Our grandfather used them for communication, true, but he never asked if those he spoke with were from this dimension or another. And they spoke in concepts, not in languages, which left neither side informed of precise locations or chronologies."

I sat up straighter. "So you reached through that same focus that brought the ship into our world and pulled through a part of the fabric of that other! I see. Ingenious. I would be greatly interested in the way in which that was done."

She laughed aloud. "Why do you think you are here?"

"Why, because of Carl's head! Through my own folly, I made it disappear, and I was honor-bound to return him to his natural state."

"If that had not happened, something else would have," she said. "Father has had great plans for you since you were born. His training is the finest in Garetha. Not even the Visionaries deny that fact. And he, in return, needs help with the younglings. The lack of a woman's hand is apparent in all the household affairs."

"You do not live here, then?"

"Heaven forfend! I have my own home and family, a less demanding one by far than this! My spouse is understanding of an absence now and then; but he knows, as I do, that our three young ones are better cared for when I am at home. No, I have children older than Nollie. My hand has been absent from my father's affairs since I was something near your own age. We talk frequently, by our own methods, and he consults with me on many occasions, but he needs one here and now to help. You can see that Nollie, alone, needs constant monitoring."

"I can, indeed," I said, recalling the tousled and unexpected apparition of the night before. "Are you all—I do not wish to offend—but are all your father's children magicians?"

She sighed and brushed a golden curl away from her cheek. "Indeed, yes. And that is a thing that is miraculous to think upon. How so many have grown even so large as the youngest without destroying themselves, our home, or the entire range of the Mountains of Myrthion I really cannot comprehend. The mischiefs of an ordinary child, though I have known very few, could not possibly perpare you for those that we could and can find to get into. Unintentionally, of course. Never maliciously. I must say that all of us of Oreon's get are good-tempered, in the main. Which is a most fortunate thing, indeed."

I sipped the glass of wine that she had handed to me,

thinking over the entire strange sequence of events since I left my home. Within the span of a year, I had grown from a rebellious daughter, a farmhand well-content to remain such, to what? A would-be sorceress. An independent, free-spirited wanderer. A boiler of witches. A castrator of lechers. A beheader of beings from another space and time. A demon's-bane. And something else. I had joined with the source, even if for so brief a time. Nothing could ever daunt me again. If the wolock had devoured me, there upon the mountainside, I would have gone into their bellies whole and untainted by unbecoming terror. And I would have then gone free—back to that source? The thought was exciting.

I had not realized that I was staring away into space as I thought, but I found my eyes focusing upon Lord Oreon, who stood beside his daughter's stool.

"Not yet, child. Not yet! The source is for those who have accomplished their life-goals, not for those intoxicated with its beauty and peace. You have hardly begun to know what it is that you do NOT know. There is a universe of skills to choose from. There are multitudes of tasks that only you will be capable of doing. There is a life for you to live, here upon Garetha, before you take wing for less finite places. I have waited many years to take you as my pupil. Would you deny me the satisfaction of seeing you upon your way?"

I looked into his merry eyes, so like Nollie's. "And in return you want my help with your family. Knowing that I refused something very similar, back in Sundoth a year past."

"Was it? Really, was it similar? Think of those mannerless children, that ungracious father."

I thought back to the spring past. I saw again those rampaging young ones making chaos of my father's hall. That grudging old man with his eyes fixed upon anything except my face. I laughed.

"You are in the right. It is not at all similar. For there sit Nollie's five siblings, curious and interested but silent as birds on a branch. And there are those just older, going quietly about their household tasks, though they must be straining to hear our words. And Agiswis, who has put me at ease, and that one who must be Thellar, leaning against the wall-hanging, grinning at me as if we had known one another all our lives. I feel at home here. As if I had come home."

Carl had finished his porridge and now came from the table to stand beside the head of the settle. His cap cocked inquiringly.

"Before we have Old Home Week, might we just see about returning my head?" His voice was good-natured but determined.

Thellar stood straight and looked at his sister. She, in turn, looked toward their father.

"Well said. I had let my mind wander, my friend. But before we restore what is lost, I need to know one thing: do you wish to retain the clarity of thought that accompanies the present transparency of your skull and its appurtenances? No matter what the continuum, such clarity is an uncomfortable thing to have. It leads to much frustration when dealing with your own kind, I must warn you. Yet it can be preserved, if you would like to have it so."

The cap-button gleamed thoughtfully. Then it nodded, once, decisively. "I would. I have learned things that I do not wish to lose—or learn to doubt. Though it has been difficult and sometimes dangerous, I am grateful to you for your experiment, Lord Oreon. My shipmates may find me changed. My superiors may doubt my report. But I wouldn't want to lose the things I have gained here."

Oreon looked pleased. "It is good to know that in my unthinking folly I have not done entirely ill. It was irresponsible, I see now, to reach forth from my own dimension and drag forth any chance comer from another. I had not thought past my own curiosity concerning the workability of my theory. I beg that you will pardon me. And now we shall return your head." He turned to look down at me.

"Grittel? Would you do the honors?"

I looked at him in astonishment. "After what I did before? I might do lasting damage!"

"Oh, no. This time you will have guidance. Thellar, see to that."

I felt a light touch, inside my mind. Something like a thought, something like a clue, something like nothing that I had ever felt. Suddenly I knew exactly where I had gone wrong in choosing a spell for Carl. Equally suddenly, I knew what I must do to put things right.

I felt something like the security that I had known when joined with the source. Closing my eyes, I thought of Carl's face as I had seen it first. I concentrated upon that, while on another level deliberately seeking to leave his mind unaffected. It seemed a long time before I opened my eyes again. Carl's living face was staring into mine.

"Did you do it?" he asked cautiously.

I nodded, and the Lord Oreon's family repeated the motion.

"You can see me now, just as I was? No beauty, but all there and visible?"

"Yes, we all can," I replied. "How do you feel?"

He looked down at himself, as if that, too, had disappeared for a time. He shook his head, touched his face, squinched his eyes. "Fine. No problem. Everything inside just as I wanted it to be. Everything on the outside in place. Seeable, I hope. Do you have a mirror?"

Thellar took down a glass from the wall and handed it to him. He observed his face closely, turning his head from side to side as if to be certain that all of it was now visible.

Handing the mirror again to Thellar, he turned to Oreon. "Now that is what I call a job worth traveling a long hard way after. Thank you, sir."

"But it was Grittel who did it. She could have done it to begin with, if she had realized how."

"Be that as it may, it happened beneath your roof and under your supervision. She wouldn't have dared to try alone. But now I need to get back to my ship. My people must be worried about me. I may be a bit stern with them, but they need me and I need them. Can you . . . do anything about that?" He looked a bit abashed, as if asking something not quite proper.

Oreon smiled widely. "Instantly!" he cried.

And where Carl had stood, there was nothing at all. I sighed. Goodbyes were, after all, sad things. I wished him well, knowing that he was, even now, greeting his crew beside their ship.

"They can make it work, now?" I asked the sorcerer.

"As soon as they have all in readiness, I will release the Spelling, and the bit of their own dimension will snap back into place. There will be no time lost from their journey, for I managed to curve it backward a bit. They will arrive on schedule. I only hope that Carl is . . . judicious . . . in speaking of this side-journey. I should hate to think of his being ridiculed. Or worse."

I thought of the sturdy comrade who had stood beside me to face the demon. Never once had he shown anything but good sense. I shook my head.

"You can trust Carl to be wise. Now. Before, I wouldn't have taken a bet on the matter."

I felt a warmth against my side and looked down to see Nollie again cuddled against me.

"You *are* going to stay, aren't you?" he asked in his grown-up way. "We all want for you to. Very, very much!"

I put an arm about his plump body. Five small faces appeared over the back of the settle. I scooted over and gestured, and they lined up along my length, sitting carefully so as not to hurt my damaged leg. Six small magicians in need of a mother-figure.

Agiswis stood abruptly and smiled. "Thank goodness!" she said. "I shall return for your wedding!" And she was gone.

I looked up, amazed, at Thellar and Oreon. "To whom?" I asked, in utter astonishment.

"Whichever of us can win your heart," they said in unison.

The leg twinged as a round bottom nudged it. I sank back on the cushions, suddenly weary past enduring.

I yawned widely. "Well, you can start tomorrow. Right now I need someone to take me to a bed so that I can sleep the clock around. Then we'll see."

The roomful of people laughed. I felt myself lifted, without the use of hands, and borne away as lightly as if I had been a featherweight. A big couch waited, its coverings turned back. My clothing peeled off, along with the layering of grime from my journey. A ruffled nightgown slid over my head, and I was lowered into the bed. The covers rolled up over me.

I sighed and straightened myself. The leg was free of its bindings! It didn't hurt at all!

It was going to be very convenient, belonging to a family of magicians.